MURDER BY SUICIDE

Volume 10: Zen and the Art of Investigation

ANTHONY WOLFF

authorHOUSE®

AuthorHouse™
1663 Liberty Drive
Bloomington, IN 47403
www.authorhouse.com
Phone: 1-800-839-8640

This is a work of fiction. All of the characters, names, incidents, organizations, and dialogue in this novel are either the products of the author's imagination or are used fictitiously.

Published by AuthorHouse 06/03/2014

ISBN: 978-1-4969-1666-2 (sc)
ISBN: 978-1-4969-1665-5 (e)

PREFACE

WHO ARE THESE DETECTIVES ANYWAY?

"'The eye cannot see itself" an old Zen adage informs us. The Private I's in these case files count on the truth of that statement. People may be self-concerned, but they are rarely self-aware.

In courts of law, guilt or innocence often depends upon its presentation. Juries do not - indeed, they may not - investigate any evidence in order to test its veracity. No, they are obliged to evaluate only what they are shown. Private Investigators, on the other hand, are obliged to look beneath surfaces and to prove to their satisfaction - not the court's - whether or not what appears to be true is actually true. The Private I must have a penetrating eye.

Intuition is a spiritual gift and this, no doubt, is why *Wagner & Tilson, Private Investigators* does its work so well.

At first glance the little group of P.I.s who solve these often baffling cases seem different from what we (having become familiar with video Dicks) consider "sleuths." They have no oddball sidekicks. They are not alcoholics. They get along well with cops.

George Wagner is the only one who was trained for the job. He obtained a degree in criminology from Temple University in Philadelphia and did exemplary work as a investigator with the Philadelphia Police. These were his golden years. He skied; he danced; he played tennis; he had a Porche, a Labrador retriever, and a small sailboat. He got married and had a wife, two toddlers, and a house. He was handsome and well built, and he had great hair.

And then one night, in 1999, he and his partner walked into an ambush. His partner was killed and George was shot in the left knee and in his right shoulder's brachial plexus. The pain resulting from his injuries and the twenty-two surgeries he endured throughout the year that followed, left him addicted to a nearly constant morphine drip. By the time he was admitted to a rehab center in Southern California for treatment of his morphine addiction and for physical therapy, he had lost everything previously mentioned except his house, his handsome face, and his great hair.

His wife, tired of visiting a semi-conscious man, divorced him and married a man who had more than enough money to make child support payments unnecessary and, since he was the jealous type, undesirable. They moved far away, and despite the calls George placed and the money and gifts he sent, they soon tended to regard him as non-existent. His wife did have an orchid collection which she boarded with a plant nursery, paying for the plants' care until he was able to accept them. He gave his brother his car, his tennis racquets, his skis, and his sailboat.

At the age of thirty-four he was officially disabled, his right arm and hand had begun to wither slightly from limited use, a frequent result of a severe injury to that nerve center. His knee, too, was troublesome. He could not hold it in a bent position for an extended period of time; and when the weather was bad or he had been standing for too long, he limped a little.

George gave considerable thought to the "disease" of romantic love and decided that he had acquired an immunity to it. He would never again be vulnerable to its delirium. He did not realize that the gods of love regard such pronouncements as hubris of the worst kind and, as such, never allow it to go unpunished. George learned this lesson while working on the case, *The Monja Blanca*. A sweet girl, half his age and nearly half his weight, would fell him, as he put it, "as young David slew the big dumb Goliath." He understood that while he had no future with her, his future would be filled with her for as long as he had a mind that could think. She had been the victim of the most vicious swindlers he had ever encountered. They had successfully fled the country, but not the range of George's determination to apprehend them. These were master criminals, four of them, and he secretly vowed that he would make them fall, one by one. This was a serious quest. There was nothing quixotic about George Roberts Wagner.

While he was in the hospital receiving treatment for those fateful gunshot wounds, he met Beryl Tilson.

Beryl, a widow whose son Jack was then eleven years old, was working her way through college as a nurse's aid when she tended George. She had met him previously when he delivered a lecture on the curious differences between aggravated assault and attempted murder, a not uninteresting topic. During the year she tended him, they became friendly enough for him to communicate with her during the year he was in rehab. When he returned to Philadelphia, she picked him up at the airport, drove him home - to a house he had not been inside for two years - and helped him to get settled into a routine with the house and the botanical spoils of his divorce.

After receiving her degree in the Liberal Arts, Beryl tried to find a job with hours that would permit her to be home when her son came home from school each day. Her quest was daunting. Not only was a degree in Liberal Arts regarded as a 'negative' when considering an applicant's qualifications, (the choice of study having demonstrated a lack of foresight for eventual entry into the commercial job market) but by stipulating that she needed to be home no later than 3:30 p.m. each day, she further discouraged personnel managers from putting out their company's welcome mat. The supply of available jobs was somewhat limited.

Beryl, a Zen Buddhist and karate practitioner, was still doing part-time work when George proposed that they open a private investigation agency. Originally he had thought she would function as a "girl friday" office manager; but when he witnessed her abilities in the martial arts, which, at that time, far exceeded his, he agreed that she should function as a 50-50 partner in the agency, and he helped her through the licensing procedure. She quickly became an excellent marksman on the gun range.

As a Christmas gift he gave her a Beretta to use alternately with her Colt semi-automatic.

The Zen temple she attended was located on Germantown Avenue in a two storey, store-front row of small businesses. Wagner & Tilson, Private Investigators needed a home. Beryl noticed that a building in the same row was advertised for sale. She told George who liked it, bought it, and let Beryl and her son move into the second floor as their residence. Problem solved.

While George considered himself a man's man, Beryl did not see herself as a woman's woman. She had no female friends her own age. None. Acquaintances, yes. She enjoyed warm relationships with a few older women. But Beryl, it surprised her to realize, was a man's woman. She liked men, their freedom to move, to create, to discover, and that inexplicable wildness that came with their physical presence and strength. All of her senses found them agreeable; but she had no desire to domesticate one. Going to sleep with one was nice. But waking up with one of them in her bed? No. No. No. Dawn had an alchemical effect on her sensibilities. "Colors seen by candlelight do not look the same by day," said Elizabeth Barrett Browning, to which Beryl replied, "Amen."

She would find no occasion to alter her orisons until, in the course of solving a missing person's case that involved sexual slavery in a South American rainforest, a case called *Skyspirit*, she met the Surinamese Southern District's chief criminal investigator. Dawn became conducive to romance. But, as we all know, the odds are always against the success of long distance love affairs. To be stuck in one continent and love a man who is stuck in another holds as much promise for high romance as falling in love with Dorian Gray. In her professional life, she was tough but fair. In matters of lethality, she preferred *dim mak* points to bullets, the latter being awfully messy.

Perhaps the most unusual of the three detectives is Sensei Percy Wong. The reader may find it useful to know a bit more about his background.

Sensei, Beryl's karate master, left his dojo to go to Taiwan to become a fully ordained Zen Buddhist priest in the Ummon or Yun Men lineage in which he was given the Dharma name Shi Yao Feng. After studying advanced martial arts in both Taiwan and China, he returned to the U.S. to teach karate again and to open a small Zen Buddhist temple - the temple that was down the street from the office *Wagner & Tilson* would eventually open.

Sensei was quickly considered a great martial arts' master not because, as he explains, "I am good at karate, but because I am better at advertising it." He was of Chinese descent and had been ordained in China, and since China's Chan Buddhism and Gung Fu stand in polite rivalry to Japan's Zen Buddhism and Karate, it was most peculiar to find a priest in China's Yun Men lineage who followed the Japanese Zen liturgy and the martial arts discipline of Karate.

It was only natural that Sensei Percy Wong's Japanese associates proclaimed that his preferences were based on merit, and in fairness to them, he did not care to disabuse them of this notion. In truth, it was Sensei's childhood rebellion against his tyrannical faux-Confucian father that caused him to gravitate to the Japanese forms. Though both of his parents had emigrated from China, his father decried western civilization even as he grew rich exploiting its freedoms and commercial opportunities. With draconian finesse he imposed upon his family the cultural values of the country from which he had fled for his life. He seriously believed that while the rest of the world's population might have come out of Africa, Chinese men came out of heaven. He did not know or care where Chinese women originated so long as they kept their proper place as slaves.

His mother, however, marveled at American diversity and refused to speak Chinese to her children, believing, as she did, in the old fashioned idea that it is wise to speak the language of the country in which one claims citizenship.

At every turn the dear lady outsmarted her obsessively sinophilic husband. Forced to serve rice at every meal along with other mysterious creatures obtained in Cantonese Chinatown, she purchased two Shar Peis that, being from Macau, were given free rein of the dining room. These dogs, despite their pre-Qin dynasty lineage, lacked a discerning palate and proved to be gluttons for bowls of fluffy white stuff. When her husband retreated to his rooms, she served omelettes and Cheerios, milk instead of tea, and at dinner, when he was not there at all, spaghetti instead of chow mein. The family home was crammed with gaudy enameled furniture and torturously carved teak; but on top of the lion-head-ball-claw-legged coffee table, she always placed a book which illustrated the elegant simplicity of such furniture designers as Marcel Breuer; Eileen Gray; Charles Eames; and American Shakers. Sensei adored her; and loved to hear her relate how, when his father ordered her to give their firstborn son a Chinese name; she secretly asked the clerk to record indelibly the name "Percy" which she mistakenly thought was a very American name. To Sensei, if she had named him Abraham Lincoln Wong, she could not have given him a more Yankee handle.

Preferring the cuisines of Italy and Mexico, Sensei avoided Chinese food and prided himself on not knowing a word of Chinese. He balanced this ignorance by an inability to understand Japanese and, because of its inaccessibility, he did not eat Japanese food.

The Man of Zen who practices Karate obviously is the adventurous type; and Sensei, staying true to type, enjoyed participating in Beryl's and George's investigations. It required little time for him to become a one-third partner of the team. He called himself, "the ampersand in *Wagner & Tilson.*"

Sensei Wong may have been better at advertising karate than at performing it, but this merely says that he was a superb huckster for the discipline. In college he had studied civil engineering; but he also was on the fencing team and he regularly practiced gymnastics. He had learned yoga and ancient forms of meditation from his mother. He attained Zen's vaunted transcendental states; which he could access 'on the mat.' It was not surprising that when he began to learn karate he was already half-accomplished. After he won a few minor championships he attracted the attention of several martial arts publications that found his "unprecedented" switchings newsworthy. They imparted to him a "great master" cachet, and perpetuated it to the delight of dojo owners and martial arts shopkeepers. He did win many championships and, through unpaid endorsements and political propaganda, inspired the sale of Japanese weapons, including nunchaku and shuriken which he did not actually use.

Although his Order was strongly given to celibacy, enough wiggle room remained for the priest who found it expedient to marry or dally. Yet, having reached his mid-forties unattached, he regarded it as 'unlikely' that he would ever be romantically welded to a female, and as 'impossible' that he would be bonded to a citizen and custom's agent of the People's Republic of China - whose Gung Fu abilities challenged him and who would strike terror in his heart especially when she wore Manolo Blahnik red spike heels. Such combat, he insisted, was patently unfair, but he prayed that Providence would not level the playing field. He met his femme fatale while working on *A Case of Virga*.

Later in their association Sensei would take under his spiritual wing a young Thai monk who had a degree in computer science and a flair for acting. Akara Chatree, to whom Sensei's master in Taiwan would give the name Shi Yao Xin, loved Shakespeare; but his father - who came from one of Thailand's many noble families - regarded his son's desire to become an actor as we would regard our son's desire to become a hit man. Akara's brothers were all businessmen and professionals; and as the old patriarch lay dying, he exacted a promise from his tall 'matinee-idol' son that he would never tread upon the flooring of a stage. The old man had asked for nothing else, and since he bequeathed a rather large sum of money to his young son, Akara had to content himself with critiquing the performances of actors who were less filially constrained than he. As far as romance is concerned, he had not thought too much about it until he worked on *A Case of Industrial Espionage*. That case took him to Bermuda, and what can a young hero do when he is captivated by a pretty girl who can recite Portia's lines with crystalline insight while lying beside him on a white beach near a blue ocean?

But his story will keep...

MONDAY, MARCH 19, 2012

The more the cold weather persisted in Philadelphia, the more Beryl Tilson was inclined to sit at her desk and stare out the office window at the drab street scene. She would seem to be studying the lifeless remnants of the season, the once-white snow that had softened to slush and then hardened into icy crust, peppered grey with the charred exhaust from tail pipes and other bits of city dirt.

The dreary days increasingly made her think of the opening of *The Wizard of Oz*. Black and white's dismal sameness; and then, in some whirlwind of memory, she'd be set down in Suriname with all its luscious color and novelty. Someone happy in her mind would say, "We're not in Kansas, anymore." And the adventure would begin.

On this morning, behind the vacant stare, she was looking out the window of a Piper Cherokee as it flew low over the Suriname River just where it bifurcates into its Gran and Pikin Tributaries. They were heading south-southwest following the Gran Rio towards Cajana, and Jan Osterhaus had his arm around her and his face next to hers as he leaned toward the window to point out some interesting feature in the rain forest.

Usually, at such times, the mailman would come to the door or the phone would ring and she would be rocketed back to the world of black and white. But on this day when the phone rang she was able to recall the dazzling colors of the parrots and the orchids and the insanely blue water of Lake Bloomenstein. She said, "Wagner and Tilson" as usual, but the voice that replied was Jan's. The adventure continued.

He tried to sound professional. "Don't get it in your head that I'm stalking you by phone... or that I'm exaggerating some flimsy reason just

1

to hear your voice again," he said with mock severity. "Don't entertain romantic nonsense of that sort. I'm not sitting here thinking about you... here... on the beach... on the river... in my bed." He sighed. "This happens to be a business call and I won't let you distort it into anything else."

"Captain Osterhaus. I'm clicking my red shoes together. Should I kick them off?"

"Yes. I'm not sure of what 'red shoes' mean, but in the words of that great wanna-be Dutch architect, Mies Van Der Rohe, 'Less is more.' Shoes are a good start. How are you, my love?"

"Bored but well. And you?"

"Lonely."

"How are things in Cajana?"

"Last I heard everything's fine. The roadhouses are legit... as far as roadhouses can ever be legit. The people are all law-abiding citizens. This time I'm the one who's on the verge of committing a capital crime. Are you interested in taking on a new case?"

"How could I not be? What's the problem?"

"It's one of those ugly family stories, and I'm too close to the parties to gain a perspective. My father's second wife, Helena Osterhaus, is driving me nuts. Are you sure you feel like listening... and remember... if you do listen to me spill my guts you'll have to come down here for a few weeks at least. You can't say, 'I can recommend a good P.I. to you.'"

"So if I let you spill your guts I'll have to go all the way down there to clean up the mess? What an image!"

Osterhaus laughed. "Good. Lighten my bloody mood. I'm sick to death with the problem. OK... here goes. You know my father was a big blonde Dutchman... more like a Viking type. A gold prospector. My mom was an aboriginal lady. To look at me is to see the mix. I can't say that I ever lost touch with my old man, because, frankly, I never was *in* touch with him. My grandparents in Amsterdam saw to it that I received a good education; and that I am the world's most brilliant investigator is *their* doing, but that I became the loving and thoughtful guy I am is due to the influence of my mom and her family. What have you learned from this that suggests you ought to marry me?"

"That I'd have a Viking for a father-in-law? God... that's such a 'turn-on'!"

"It probably would be except the old man died last year... in prison."

"Bollocks."

"God help me," he whispered. "Ok. Once again. I'll try to explain my peculiar family history. Try to listen without making me laugh. I am being harassed by his widow. All right. Here goes." He sighed again. "My mom died young and dear old dad got himself another gal... a German lady, Greta Gerber, who had three kids. He didn't marry her and he didn't have any kids by her, but they lived together here in Paramaribo for years.

"My dad made quite a few guilders panning gold, so money is involved. Greta was a divorcee. Two of her kids were teenagers and the third was a baby who had a learning disability of some kind. Everything was fine for a couple of years until, one summer day about fifteen or so years ago, my grandparents showed up with a very marriageable second cousin in tow."

"A Vikette?"

Jan laughed. "Only on the inside. Outwardly she was dainty and much younger than dear old dad. Helena. She's the one who is driving me nuts.

"My dad went to Amsterdam and married her and had two daughters. He'd come back here regularly to attend to business and he always stayed with Greta - whose bills he always paid. After three years of living in Amsterdam he came back for good. He didn't like Amsterdam society and Helena didn't like our tropical paradise. They never divorced, and he paid her bills, too.

"He continued prospecting and panning, and he must have had a knack for hitting the right streams. He was very secretive about his destinations; but he managed to live very well here and, as I've said, he sent money home to his family in Amsterdam.

"One day in October 2008, Greta's kids, Dolph and Andrea, who were working adults - the youngest one, Juliana, was a teenager in a special school -anyway, Dolph and Andrea came home from spending a

couple of days with their friends for the October 3rd holiday, Hutspot...
what you call Hodge Podge Day. They were not together but they came
home minutes apart. Dolph saw his mother's car parked in the street,
so he assumed she was home. He called her, but she didn't answer. He
hollered out the back door. No answer. Andrea pulls up. They go from
room to room and then search the back yard. Andrea sees a bit of fabric
sticking out of the dirt where three rose bushes have just been planted. It
was the end of an apron string. They pull it and find Greta's body buried
under the bushes.

"A bullet had been fired into her right temple. They called the police.
Powder burns indicated a contact wound. Greta's hand and arm bore no
trace of gun shot residue. She had been shot with a .25 caliber weapon
and my father was known to have such a gun although it was nowhere in
the house or yard. Metal detectors were used to scour the grounds. So
it was evident that someone had held a gun to her head and fired it, put
her body in a trench that had been recently dug for the roses and then
hastily planted the roses on top of her.

"My father claimed to be with a few 'biker chicks' and yes... we have
a few motorcycle clubs down here too... and before you ask... they drive
Harleys. Most are decent law-abiding people, but a few are the renegade
gang type. He tested positive for cocaine in his system, but he couldn't
locate the girls he was snorting it with to help him with an alibi - maybe
they just didn't want to get involved in a police matter."

"How old was he and, by the way, what was his name?"

"Sixty-three when he died, and his name was Piet. He was fifty-
nine when this happened. He had no alibi. He had been heard arguing
with Greta about a new will he had written. He left his European
property - mostly a few houses and a bank account - to Helena and
his two daughters. Greta got the lion's share of his assets, yet it was
determined that they were arguing about the will... which doesn't make
a lot of sense. With no alibi, with the slug in Greta's head matching the
slugs he had fired into a tree for target practice, and with the argument
on record, he was charged and convicted. We don't have a jury system
and the judges tried to be fair.

"Piet had high blood pressure and the strain of incarceration was too much on him, I guess. He already had a stroke a few years before; but he was a stubborn man and didn't take proper care of himself. He claimed to be completely innocent. He had no friends and nobody except one of Greta's kids - Andrea - believed him. Finally, a blood vessel burst in his head and he died suddenly in prison."

"Why didn't he have friends?"

"He wasn't what you'd call 'a nice man.' Prospectors tend to be tough, solitary, and suspicious of everyone. Friends often turn out to be claim jumpers. Business labs will issue fake assay reports. That's what they worry about. Solitude is fine if you're an ascetic - a religious recluse. But he was hardly that."

"Why did you say that the grave roses were hastily planted?"

"The apron string stuck out and also the roots of the rose bushes had not been completely covered. Without her body in the trench that had been dug for the roses, they would have been lower and the excavated dirt and potting soil around them would have covered them. As it was, some roots were showing."

"What did Greta leave her family?"

"I didn't know any of this until the trial, but apparently he was a cagey guy who didn't believe in contracts or wills or any kind of legal document that the testimony of liars and forgers could get a court to overturn. Prospectors tend to be away from home for long stretches, and Greta did have a head for business and could make quick decisions. His businesses started small but really grew. The talk was that he would make Greta the owner of a property or business and then lend her money for household and business expenses, using the property or business as collateral, so that she was always in debt to him. She couldn't sell anything because he always had these liens against everything... plus her promissory notes. I don't know what he was up to. When she died, her heirs inherited her ownership and I don't know what happened to the documents that indebted her to him. Those documents were assets of his; but he never produced them."

"Are you saying that he was convicted of murdering her yet he never filed the liens against the properties, preventing her children from inheriting? If the debts were greater than the value of the properties, his wife and kids would have gotten ownership. I don't understand. He paid Helena's bills in Amsterdam, but he didn't want her to inherit anything in Suriname?"

"That's it, exactly. He had a fleet of helicopters and single engine aircraft that he leased to various businesses and individuals - often supplying the pilots if they didn't have one of their own. Dolph got that business. He also had a miners' supply company which sold small items and leased some heavy excavation machinery - backhoes and bulldozers, that sort of thing. Andrea and her husband got that business. He had real estate in Suriname, Colombia, and elsewhere. And, of course, he had those maps to his secret gold mining sites. Greta's kids got it all... unencumbered.

"The residence - they call it Gerber House - was a little different. He had ordered it to be built and titled to her alone; but he acted as a contractor for additional work that was done, and then he filed a lien against it, so that she was never able to sell it. She had no income of her own. She also signed promissory notes using the house as collateral. Those documents were executed in a bank. It was all legitimate. The debts had been recorded against her home, but Andrea hired an attorney for him and before the trial was over he had withdrawn them all as having been satisfied. So her children also got clear title to the house."

"How long had Greta been dead?"

"The medical examiner got there at 6 p.m. He said thirty hours plus or minus the usual cover-your-ass allowance."

"And did that absolutely rule out Dolph, Andrea, and Juliana?"

"Yes. None was anywhere near Paramaribo at the time of her death."

"When the neighborhood was canvassed, did anyone report hearing a shot fired?"

"No... but it was a holiday and some people get rowdy."

"Was another woman involved?"

"No. None. Neither of them had any love interest on the side."

"I'm curious about why Greta would argue about the disposition of his estate."

"I couldn't understand it either. I didn't know her well - hardly at all, in fact. But what I knew of her, she was the sweet and obedient hausfrau type. I had a hard time imagining that they had ever argued about anything. He was a dictator who didn't believe in parliamentary procedures."

"What about Juliana?"

"She was left out of the record. Psychologically, she wasn't in a position to manage her own money. I assume that her care was left up to her brother and sister."

"Then why were they fighting? If he had reached that much of an accord with her, why would he risk murdering her? Why murder her at all? I don't see 'motive.' If he had all those IOU's and liens to file, he could have come forward with them and ruined her financially. When people reported that they had argued, were they sure it was about money?"

Jan hesitated. "Let me look through the file." He shuffled papers and then read, muttering in Dutch, which he translated. "It was definitely about money; but none of the neighbors was able to get details. When my grandparents in Amsterdam came to make a statement, they alluded to the new will. He discussed it with them on the phone. They didn't like it and thought they had persuaded him to change it back to favoring his wife. That, then, became the assumption: he and Greta fought about revising the new will. In the heat of passion he shot her. He had a temper and everyone knew it."

"Heat of passion? Who dug the trench?"

"He denied digging it, but her hands bore no evidence of blistering which, considering the amount of dirt that had been removed, would have had to be present. So he was considered the digger."

"I can see 'sweat of exertion' in that climate, but not 'heat of passion.' Nobody just happens to dig a grave for his victim and then gets angry and kills her. That, by definition, is premeditated."

"The thought was that he dug the trench for the roses and then used it as a convenient grave. Then he lied and said he didn't have anything to do with the grave."

"What did the autopsy reveal... and the forensics?"

"The lividity indications were where they should be. She was killed and immediately dumped in the trench. That the grave was sloppily finished was considered proof of his drugged state. There was no weapon, so she didn't kill herself. The slug matched the slugs of a weapon he owned. No GSR. He was convicted and sentenced to what was tantamount to a life sentence. Twenty years. As I've said, three years later he died. My grandparents immediately advised Helena not to fight over his assets but instead to press for the restoration of his good name. Helena still is determined to clear his name. His daughters - who are my half-sisters - are approaching marriageable age and nothing can ruin a girl's hopes for a good match like having a murderer hanging on the paternal tree. Every few months I'd get a phone call or a letter asking me what I've done to clear my father's good name. Now, suddenly, the urgency is such that they've come here. I'm told they're in town, but I haven't talked to them yet. All three of them... Helena and the girls. I had promised that I'd call in a private investigator. And here I am. What do you think?"

"Just from what you're telling me it doesn't make a whole lot of sense. If Greta got the lion's share, why would she argue? If he threatened to revise the will in favor of Helena, then it might make sense if Greta *shot him*. If Piet didn't want Greta or her heirs to have his property, he'd have filed the liens.

"He's a prospector who digs for gold but does a sloppy job of burying his murder victim? A man who is secretive about his gold panning places but leaves his murder victim in the back yard? A man who lives with a woman in apparent harmony, and has no children with her yet provides well for her children and gives little to his own? And why would a man who already had a stroke kill the one person who would be his nurse if he had another one? Why would a man who already had one stroke dig such a trench for rose bushes at all? He had money. He'd hire someone! Did they look for a worker Greta could have hired?"

"Yes, they looked. But no one was found. She had never hired such help before, so they didn't give that possibility much weight. Piet denied knowing anything about the roses or the trench. I've got the official photos of the crime scene I can send you. It'll give you something to look at while you're flying down here."

"I think you need answers... better answers than the ones you've been given. Incidentally, were you mentioned in the will?"

"No. He and I had a falling out some ten years ago. I didn't like the man - and he didn't like me."

"And now his widow Helena and her daughters are in Paramaribo determined that his name be cleared." Beryl sighed. "Three years later? Did anything unusual happen in the last three years?"

"Not that I know of. She says it is because her girls are teenagers now and it's having a negative effect on their social life. She thinks I can just pull a few strings and clear him. I can't do it. I have washed my 'mental hands' of the whole business. I don't like Helena and I didn't know Greta. The crime wasn't committed in my jurisdiction and it would be an insult to my colleagues to stick my nose in an investigation they conducted. I am interested only because it is a great way to get a certain P.I. down here."

"Since you put it that way, I cannot refuse. I'll be your own personal sleuth. Ok. Email me the CSP and I'll look at them on my way down. It's difficult to imagine such a bizarre burial scene."

"I'll have a ticket reserved for you at KLM's counter. How soon?"

"I've got to get things in order, so I'll make my own reservations. Will we have to go into the bush?"

"No, it all happened here in Paramaribo... unless you want to travel with a certain National Investigation Bureau captain down to Brokopondo... or down the Suriname River all the way to the rapids... or even down into Brazilian territory where we'd never be heard from again... except in legends."

"Sounds like a plan. I'll make my reservations for tomorrow and call you back with flight details. Get all the files together... her autopsy... his autopsy... all the forensic studies... all her financial records and medical records as well as his... and make sure we have access to the crime scene."

"Yes, Ma'am. *Tot morgen!*"

Beryl made reservations, closed the office, called her hairdresser, and having only two hours' time until her appointment, went out to the mall to get something new and exciting to wear. She also notified George Wagner and Sensei Percy Wong that she'd probably be using the cover of a "free lance journalist" working on a South American Gold Rush feature for Burnham Publications. They kept a phone line in the office dedicated to spurious employments.

Life was no longer black, white, grey and dreary.

TUESDAY, MARCH 20, 2012.

It was late in the afternoon when the Boeing 757 touched down at Pengel International Airport. Beryl had only carry-on luggage. She remembered the shops in Paramaribo... the silk saris... the couturier fashions in the hotels. She'd buy her clothing "as needed."

As she cleared customs she could see Jan waiting at the gate. He said nothing to her as she approached. They did not kiss or exchange greetings. Instead, as onlookers observed, they appeared to be two thin clay people who were attempting to become one stout one. She dropped her bags at her side and the two of them wrapped their arms around each other and squeezed for an inexcusably long time. "Get a room!" a man muttered as he passed, and the two of them finally let go to burst out laughing.

"Arrest him!" Beryl said.

"I ought to," Jan said. "He was interfering with a police investigation."

Jan had exercised the perquisite of office and parked in a no-parking zone. As they walked to his Land Rover people looked at them quizzically. "This doesn't look like 'official business,'" Beryl quipped. "The least you could have done was handcuff me."

"That comes later," Jan said. Again they laughed.

"You are a beast," she said. "Before it gets dark, take me to the crime scene."

"Jesus. You don't waste time with preliminaries!"

"Where I come from, we know that where you're coming from, that is called 'foreplay.' Drive!"

11

The Gerber House had an individual charm on the street that was so thickly lined with trees that it required an effort to see the individual charm of other houses. Each house was unique, yet they all seemed to be connected by the rows of symphonia trees that flanked both sides of the wide avenue.

The house had an old medieval look to it. The front was completely flat from doorstep to the top of the gable, the plastered walls were tan, the windows, shutters, and the planks that secured the structure's facade like so many seams were all dark natural walnut, and the roof was enameled red clay tiles. Painted earthenware pots that were filled with blooming flowers lined the front of the house as it met the sidewalk. Both sides of the house were gated: a narrow one for an alley used to deliver trash cans to the street; and a wide sliding gate on the other that barred entrance to the side lawn and the entire rear garden.

"Is this the house your father bought for Greta?" Beryl asked.

"Yes. They lived in it for some fifteen or sixteen years."

"Did he have it built for her? The reason I ask is that it has a decided old German look to it."

"As a matter of fact, he did have it built to spec. An architect, who's dead now, designed it. There's one large room attached to the rear. My father built that after if was finished."

"Who lives here now?"

"Adolph 'Dolph' Gerber is the man of the house. He's in his thirties. He's Greta's only son. Her other two kids are daughters."

"Three kids..." she teased. "One was a son and the other two are... daughters? Funny, how when you really put your mind to it--"

Jan pretended to get her in a choke-hold. "You're gonna get us thrown out and we haven't gotten in yet."

"I thought you set everything up."

"Look, I'm not really what you'd call a blood relation. I don't have any privileges here."

"Then let's not knock on the door. Let's just go through the side gate to get to the rear to see the infamous roses. If he stops us, say we didn't want to disturb him during his dinner hour. I'll be a free lance journalist who's doing a piece on gold prospectors in Suriname."

They had to pull on the gate to slide it open. "This makes me uncomfortable," Jan said. "I feel like it's a B&E."

"Only if it's locked. And it doesn't seem to be. Just hope that B&E doesn't stand for Biting and Eviscerating. They might be keeping a couple of rottweilers back there."

"I'll leave the gate open in case we have to make a fast getaway. I should have brought my Colt."

They followed the side entrance path back to the rear. Three sides of the property were enclosed with a cinderblock wall. The house was a square two-storey structure that had a large room built onto it on one side of the rear. The area between that room and the opposite wall could have functioned as a separate area for patio or play, but there were no flagstones, walkways, or any indications of use in the new-mown grass. It was in this section of lawn that a row of three rose bushes grew in a coffin-sized plot. "What's that room for?" Beryl asked.

"The kitchen. By letting it extend from the house it can have windows on three sides for light and ventilation. I think Greta also used it as a laundry room." He pointed to the rose bushes. "Those are probably the same roses and that's the exact place they were found. Maybe the place was chosen because as a hausfrau that's where she spent most of her time."

"What is this thing in the photos?" Jan looked over her shoulder and saw that she was pointing to a long plank that had a foot-high riser bracketed to one side of it. It was leaning against the shed in which they stored their trash cans and gardening equipment. "It looks to be the same length as the grave."

"Yes. It's a thin wooden plank... probably tropical pine... much like the skin they use on interior framed doors."

"What was it for?"

"Nobody knew. Andrea thought it might be something that Juliana played with."

They continued to walk around the property. The wall on the side they had entered formed a backdrop for a variety of flowers and shrubs. In the rear, crimson and coral colored bougainvillea cascaded over the top of the grey blocks. In the yard's corners stood trees that were fully blooming with scarlet flowers.

Beryl admired the flowering trees. "What are they? I've seen them someplace before."

"We call them marriage trees - because the scarlet flowers leave behind foot-long seed pods that fall without mercy. It is just like marriage, they say. Not like ours will be, of course, but the way theirs usually are. The tree, like love, blossoms flamboyantly, but it soon develops into something like getting hit with a rolling pin. 'Oh! The pain!' they say. The line always gets a laugh." He picked up an old foot-long seed pod and showed her.

The third wall of the garden was covered with vines that congregated at the base to form a bower of green leaves. A lawn mower had obviously kept the growth in check or it would have spread all over the lawn.

Beryl walked over to it. "This is kudzu. I could see it in the photos. I didn't know you had it down here."

"Yes. If I'm not mistaken, it's a relatively new plant to us. I think we learned from others that it's futile to try to kill it with herbicides. People pull it out, prune it, or even keep a goat on the premises to eat the stuff as it grows. People can eat it, too. I understand that in Japan it's considered a good vegetable."

"Does it dry up in the winter?" Beryl stepped through the mounds of kudzu to examine a row of poles that had been smothered by the kudzu.

"We have no winter."

Beryl looked again at the crime scene photographs Jan had sent. "I figured that these kudzu-covered poles were used for clothes-lines. All you can see clearly in the photos are the opposite poles by that... that kitchen wall." She examined the inside of the hooks at the top. "These are shiny and worn," she said, "which means they're currently being used. The paint gets rubbed off when the line is pulled taut. If it's not taut," she explained, "it'll sag and the laundry will drag on the ground." She walked to the opposite poles to check their hooks. "Yes... these are worn, too. Don't they have a clothes dryer in the house?"

"I guess they do. But in the tropics it's customary to air out rugs of every kind... wicker type rugs... wool rugs... it doesn't matter. To keep the mold from growing in them, they're usually hung outside and the backs are sprayed with bleach and left to dry in the sun. When they're put back on the floor, the bleach has a deterrent effect on insects and it prevents mold, too."

"It's an odd place to have buried Greta... here in the same space they'd hang their rugs. Roses have thorns and they'd snag anything you hung near them." She checked the photographs. "And they found her in the bottom of the grave and these three rose bushes neatly sitting on top of her?"

"I don't know how neat they were. When Dolph and Andrea found her they had the wherewithal to leave her in place and call the police. By the time the site was processed, the dirt and bushes were disturbed."

"Incidentally, do you have many moles or rats... you know... the vermin type of pest one usually finds around human habitation?"

"Like Norway rats? Sure. We have a variety of rats and mice, too. Why do you ask?"

"I'm considering an alternate scenario." She shrugged. "So the son still lives in the house momma was murdered in. That's interesting." She looked up at the house's windows. There were no lights on inside and she could not see that they were being watched by someone who was standing behind the curtain of a second storey rear window. "Ok. Let's say that Piet didn't do it. Who else would have had a motive? Has suicide ever been considered?"

"Suicide? No. Everyone said she was a happy woman. There was no reason for Greta to want to kill herself."

"None that you know of. It's a mistake to think that suicides are all despondent people trying to escape a cruel world. Sometimes they act out of concern for others. Could Greta have thought she had an incurable disease... one that would have taken up much of the family's currency and care? Was she experiencing the symptoms of dementia or any other protracted disease? Many suicides don't want their deaths to appear to be suicides. Sometimes it's a case of the stigma of suicide. A person knows he's terminally ill but doesn't want people to think his act is cowardly or has been influenced by euthanasia ideologues. He may be trying to avoid the shame of violating a religious prohibition.

"A suicide puts a lot of guilt onto family members. It is divisive; but a random murder tends to unite family members in the tragedy. You never hear a person speak well of his relationship to a suicide. Instead, it's always recriminations. 'Why didn't he come to me to talk it over? I'd have given him the money!' 'Oh, I should have invited him out to a ball game once in a while. And where were his kids? Didn't they know how lonely he was?' But a murder will get people to say, 'Oh, he was the sweetest man. He didn't have an enemy in the world. We'll all miss him so much.'

"I'm just suggesting that if she had a reason and some help, she could have committed suicide. What was she wearing?"

"That's another reason suicide was ruled out. She was wearing a housedress and an apron. She was baking cookies and bread. In fact there were trays of cookies she hadn't yet put in the oven when she was killed. A woman isn't going to kill herself in the middle of an afternoon of baking cookies."

"She isn't? And what are the allowable hours or functions in which she is permitted to conduct her suicide?"

"Ouch."

"Was there anything unusual or out of place out here? I'm having a hard time imagining a prospector burying someone and leaving a hunk of the person's clothing sticking out of the grave."

"I wondered about that, too. But the top of the grave was all potting soil and it had rained through the night, so the thought was that what had once been covered had been uncovered by the rain. There are other official photos of the crime scene. Maybe they'll reveal more to you. And they, my love, are at my apartment… which is where I think you ought to be. Haven't you seen enough for today?"

"What happened with the third child, the second daughter?"

"Juliana? She's in a special private school here. Learning disabilities or psychological problems. Only Andrea and Dolph went to the funeral and attended the trial."

"Ok. Let's go back to your place, but I want to stop at a pet shop on the way."

"You've got a theory. I can tell. What is it?"

"Not a theory. Just another explanation for the observed facts. I don't want to build up your resistance to the idea. So let's just go to the pet store. And if we pass a bakery, I want to stop there, too."

Beryl purchased a twenty-five foot long retractable leash. She noticed that there were also rats for sale in the shop, sold as food for pet snakes. There was a bakery a few stores away from the pet shop in which she purchased an unsliced loaf of white bread.

In Jan's apartment Beryl was so focussed on the task that the romantic interlude he had envisioned vanished.

"All right," she announced. "Let's proceed with the demonstration." She pulled out and discarded enough of the interior of the loaf of bread to enable her to insert her hand into it. Then she lay the hollowed loaf on the kitchen table.

Jan picked it up and stared at her. "I know where you're going with this. I know exactly where you're going with this. Let me help you." He went to a cabinet and took out a long spool of twine.

Using the twine, she tied the collar end of the leash to the bathroom shower rod and the retractable leash's handle to a can opener. She then opened the ratchet so that the leash unwound as she walked in a straight line from the bathroom into his living room.

Jan had already moved his couch so that the extended leash comfortably reached it. "And I can see that being right-handed, you'll lie on the couch with your right hand closest to the shower rod. I'm trying not to imagine rats running all over you."

She placed her right hand into the hollowed-out loaf of bread which covered her hand and arm nearly to her elbow. "Try to imagine that the strings and the loaf of bread are sugared and buttered and maybe have some kind of fragrant cheese rubbed onto them. While you're visualizing that, imagine also that I've positioned the three rose bushes on my prostrated body, and have pulled onto myself as much of the loose excavated dirt as I can. Now... let's see. I want to complete the burial so I use that thin board with its bracketed riser - which I've completely filled with dry, light-weight potting soil - and I put a rock under it so that it is tipped at, say, a 40 degree angle. I run a well-buttered and sugared string or twine from a little hole in the riser through my belt buckle - which is about the mid-point of the grave - and then down onto my foot. Maybe I bend my leg at the knee. Now, get ready." Beryl lay on the couch and said, "Pow!" She fired the can opener into her temple, and released the weapon as her leg, in a reflex action, straightened and fell, pulling on the string which caused the imagined long board filled with dry potting soil to tip over. The can-opener-gun zipped across the room and slammed against the shower rod. "This," said Beryl, "makes more sense than what the prosecution determined."

"Yes... It's as good a way to explain the events as any other theory I've heard. A suicide made to look like a murder. But why would she do it?"

"That's what the investigation's supposed to establish. Who knows what any suicidal person is thinking? He might want to make it look like murder because the death would fall within the two-year exemption of an insurance policy's suicide clause. But as we discussed, there are many motives for committing the ultimate act. And there are many clever 'means' to accomplish it.

"To keep the police from suspecting that the death was by suicide, the person can tie a helium balloon to the gun and when he or she falls over, the balloon goes up, up, and away... to come down in a lake or at sea or the middle of a desert. Sometimes a person will stand on a bridge over a fast moving river and then shoot himself and fall down into the water while the gun remains on the bridge for anyone to pick up."

"I can see it when the objective is avoiding a suicide clause in the terms of an insurance policy. But that wasn't Greta's problem. The police did look into the insurance angle. There was no policy on her life, so insurance was not a point of interest. She had not seen a doctor in several years. At autopsy, her health was determined to be perfect."

"We can't overlook what seems to be staring us in the face," Beryl warned. "And that is the possibility that the deceased might have planted evidence to cast suspicion on another individual. People can be wily and spiteful. Piet was in that wild 'middle-age crazy' phase. Motorcycles and cocaine at his age! Those pursuits accompany a need for sexual gratification. Are you sure Piet didn't meet someone? Maybe he threatened to dump Greta and move a girlfriend into the house. Well, if Greta intended to hurt Piet, she succeeded."

Jan nodded. "As unpleasant as that is to think about, it's a viable explanation. We still need to determine who removed the board and retrieved the gun," he said. "Both could have been done before Dolph and Andrea got home." He displayed another crime scene photograph. "Look!" he said. "The grave was 1.68 meters - that's five and a half feet long - and it was only a foot and a half wide."

"How tall was Greta?"

"As you might imagine... a little less than five and a half feet tall."

Beryl studied the photographs. "Yes. The rats would find their way through the loose potting soil to get to that loaf of bread and the string. They would quickly consume them, and there would be no tell-tale tipping string or gun shot residue on her hand or arm because the rats would have it all in their bellies. They could devour the whole mess in twenty minutes. If she purchased rats they could even have been helped by resident rats. It makes sense to me," Beryl said.

"Because of my relationship to the case, the guys let me see the crime scene, but it wasn't my place to ask official questions." Jan continued the theory. "The weapon, hidden high among the kudzu? That never occurred to anyone. The police would have searched the ground with metal detectors, but nobody looked for the gun up high on a pole. And kudzu grows a foot a day. Even if the gun were in full view when she shot herself, it would have been covered up by the next day. Yes, she had to have help. The gun couldn't have stayed up in the pole for long. Her children would have reported it when they found it eventually, but there was never a report.

"I stayed away from the investigation for obvious reasons. I don't know whether he was guilty or not. But I think I can say that he was convicted after some lousy police work." Jan got up and tossed the photographs onto his desk.

"Say what you will," said Beryl, "I can suck the romance out of any room in the hemisphere. Did I tell you I'm hungry?"

He reached around and grabbed her. "I am a patient man. Let's go out and get some dinner."

"Then we can talk about the mystery."

"Mystery? Which is?"

"Why she would want to kill herself and blame your father for her death."

"Sure... we can discuss it between the soup and salad. And then again after dessert. Jesus! Another two hours!"

.

Beryl did not eat soup or salad. She had sliced fruit and yogurt. For no other reason but that he did not feel like eating, Jan ate the same. "If she did do this I can think of only one motive," she said, "and that is something hateful... spite or revenge."

"Let's see," Jan said, "we'll assume she was more or less certain that he'd be blamed. If he were guilty he'd have gone to more trouble to fix his alibi unless he thought he was protecting someone... a married girlfriend? I give up. I can't think of anything that would prompt her to do it."

"Are the Amsterdam wife and kids nice people?"

"No. They're smug self-important snotty types. All three of them. They didn't show up for the trial. My grandparents were here and sat in court everyday. Andrea - Greta's daughter - stuck by Piet; but not his wife and two daughters. I went to the trial and sat in the back of the room. When reporters asked me a question, I simply said, 'No comment,' or, 'Let the law take its course.' Greta's son Dolph was there and his expression was as blank as mine. I'm a lot older than my half-sisters, so they're not in my social sphere. But Greta's kids were closer in age to me.

When we saw each other we'd nod and that was it. Did I tell you that I'm in love with you?"

"Not really... not in so many words."

"Well, I am. But you never tell me that you love me."

"I'm such an independent hag! You'll have to get me in the throes of ecstasy before I make such compromising remarks."

"I should arrest you for littering. You have thrown my heart into the gutter."

"That would be 'suspicion of littering.' You didn't actually see me throw it anywhere. And then your heart would turn up safe and sound in the pocket of some floozy... with absolutely no evidence of ever having been abused. Making false charges... that's serious stuff. How well did you know the Amsterdam people before your father's death?"

Jan sighed. "I didn't know them at all. I saw Helena when my grandparents first brought her here to meet my father, and that's it. She didn't like the tropics. I didn't see her again until he died. She came for the funeral and the reading of the will. I haven't had to deal with her until she started pestering me to clear my father's name."

"Then if you didn't see her during those years, chances are that Greta didn't see her either. No cause there for such spite. I didn't see any victimology statement in her dossier. I wish we knew more about Greta."

"There's really nothing known about her life before she moved into the house my father had built for her."

"I'm puzzled about her divorce. She's married for years and has kids who are getting ready for college; and then suddenly she gets pregnant and her husband divorces her. Then Piet Osterhaus takes her in. Is it possible that Juliana is his child?"

"Funny you should bring that up. Years ago I was discussing that possibility with a nurse I was dating. Greta had sent out Christmas cards that had a picture of her three kids in it. The person who got one of the cards knew that she was dating me and showed my nurse friend the photo; and she asked if she could borrow it for a few days to show me. When she did she asked, 'What does it mean that Juliana's eyes are brown?'

"I didn't know. I never saw Greta's husband. Then she said, 'Greta has blue eyes and so does her husband. Piet's eyes are also blue. Blue-eyed genes are recessive. Both parents have to have them and therefore they'll produce a blue-eyed child.' I looked it up and what I read supported her claim: my father could not have been Juliana's father. Yet he lived with Greta while she was pregnant. From what I understand they were supposed to get married when her divorce was final, but they never did."

"Maybe she told Piet that the baby was his and when the brown-eyed baby was born, he knew he had been duped."

"My father would have killed her. Nobody could make a fool of him. He was among the most narcissistic and vicious men I've ever known. Let's go home," he said, "and sleep on it after we have a shower."

"The two of us standing in your bathtub?"

Jan laughed. "Look... I'm a tub guy. In the tropics, you like to get your plumbing good and clean. I like baths. The shower curtain is fine. When I'm finished the bath - I'm telling you this so you'll know what to expect–" He began to laugh. "I stand up and run the shower. It's an old apartment and it has a small bathroom. I couldn't fit a stall shower into it if I wanted to. I'm happy with the tub. Now, if I knew that a certain P.I. from Philadelphia was going to share that shower with me..."

Two hours later, precisely at nine o'clock, they emerged from the bathtub shower laughing and doing towel snaps and being recklessly naked, albeit with the blinds drawn, when the door bell rang and a knock as ominous as the tolling of a death knell sounded at the door. Jan looked at Beryl quizzically. "Who is it?" he yelled as he grabbed a bathrobe for her and wrapped a towel around himself.

"Mrs. Osterhaus. Mrs. Helena Osterhaus. Would you mind terribly not leaving us out here like beggars?"

Jan looked at Beryl and whispered, "Well, fuck me! I've only waited months for this honeymoon and I'm gonna spend it playing host to Daddy's little widow?" He opened the door, yelling, "And who the hell is 'us'? My half-sisters?"

The girls giggled. Helena Osterhaus took a step towards Jan. "Who else would it be? Did you not know we were coming?" She tapped him on the chest, a gesture that had the force of a shove as he backed away from her hand.

"Arriving in Suriname and arriving at my front door are two different things," he said. "You are what in polite society is called, 'unannounced.'"

"And what, precisely, do you know about polite society?" Helena Osterhaus smiled in a saccharin way at Beryl as she led her daughters into the room. She waved her hand in announcement. "The misses Elise and Gretchen Osterhaus."

Beryl looked at the two girls who appeared to be in their teens. They had the smug look of someone who knew a great secret that no one else was qualified to hear. "I'm Beryl Tilson," Beryl said, "a private investigator from the United States."

"What are you investigating?" Helena asked, looking down at Jan's towel-wrap.

"Inasmuch as your daughters are present, I'll just excuse myself." Beryl returned to the bedroom and shut the door.

Helena Osterhaus turned to Jan, "I'm here to determine your progress in investigating the miscarriage of justice suffered by my late husband. I intend that his good name be restored. It is quite enough that we were robbed of so much of his estate. As Shakespeare said, 'He who steals my purse steals trash, but he who steals my good name...' something like that. I am not exactly an anglophile."

"I am working on the case. I have made progress. I intend to make more progress. And I also intend that you shall leave. Call my office and let my secretary know where you're staying. I will call you as soon as I have something to say. Right now I am made speechless by your lack of decorum." The door was still open. He reached for it and opened it wider, gesturing that they should leave.

The two girls smirked as they sashayed past him.

Helena waved her fingers. "We're at the Trop. No need to burden your secretary. Call me... sooner than later. I shouldn't like to have to come looking for you in your office."

"I have been warned," Jan said as he shut and bolted the door. He walked back towards the bedroom. *"Vrouw! Kom hier! Breng de handboeien en de zweep."*

The door opened and Beryl emerged laughing. "I can't speak Dutch but I bloody well know what you just said. Oh, you he-man you! *'Whip me. Beat me. Make me write bad checks.'"*

"You've been such a bad girl..." They began to laugh together. Jan slapped an empty clip into his gun. "The next person who comes to my door will not live long enough to say, 'Sorry, I've got the wrong unit.' Ground floor of a duplex? What the hell was I thinking?"

WEDNESDAY, MARCH 21, 2012.

"I admit, " Beryl said as she poured coffee at the patio breakfast table, "that we just don't know enough to account for such a spiteful act. I kept waking up last night asking myself what could possibly make a woman kill herself and try to blame somebody else for it."

"And just think... I was lying beside you wondering if anything in the world smelled as good as that ginger shampoo you used on your hair. Maybe I should see a doctor. Something must be wrong."

"I will ignore that lovely remark. Greta was in good health physically; and mentally, all the people who were interviewed insisted that she was in good spirits. She didn't have to go to work. I see photos of her house. It's well kept and has all the accoutrements of contented living... photos... a music room with a piano that a neighbor says she often played - and played well! Hand-made crocheted tablecloths and needlepoint pillow covers. An inventory of her medications shows nothing stronger than aspirin. The woman wasn't even constipated. Suicidal? Where are the indications of suicide? She had to stage this elaborate plot to get Piet blamed for her murder, but I can't see why she'd do it.

"So much was left to chance. No, *too much* was left to chance. If a person is so intent upon having someone charged and convicted of murder, there can be no loose ends. She had to have an accomplice. Yes, maybe she knew that Piet would do that night what he did every night - party with drugs. She might figure, 'Who would alibi him? No one would confess that he or she was with Piet all night snorting cocaine.' But other than that, she had to be sure that the dirt convincingly covered her, that the rats ate the bread and string, that the gun that was stuck up in the metal pole would be removed. You are going to have to go much

25

deeper into Piet and Greta's lives. Why did she do it, and who helped her to do it?"

Jan agreed. "Since it's no longer an open police case, I can dig into things. There is so much about the old man that I've never understood. His mysterious gold mining operations, for example."

"Yes, it is mysterious. He seems to have been well-off. Striking it rich panning for gold may give a man seed money to start other businesses; but you and I both know that an ordinary placer claim in an unprotected area is gonna draw claim jumpers and high graders—"

"What's a high grader?"

"You hire a man to work your claim and he finds a nice nugget and instead of giving it to you, he steals it."

"Ah, yes. Piet attributed his wealth and its replenishment to regular visits to his secret mining claim; but if the claim were *that* valuable and he didn't record it, others would record it. They'd trail him - especially in these days of GPS technology. Once someone found it, they would file a valid claim to the site, and then they'd simply guard it from him and everybody else even if they had to make its perimeter a mine field. If he went down to his mine site regularly, he might have used it as a kind of base camp and went elsewhere."

"If he had been part of a cocaine distribution system, would you be told about it?"

"Yes. Definitely," he answered quickly. "I thought about that when he was arrested and had a snout full of cocaine. I actually inquired, but I was assured that he had purchased the stuff locally. It's not likely that he'd be a conduit for cocaine and then go out and buy someone else's stuff."

Jan's phone rang. He read the caller identification. "Dolph Gerber is calling. I'm beginning to envy orphans." He answered the call.

Adolph Gerber got right to the point. "I understand that you and a woman were trespassing on my property yesterday afternoon. I'd like to know what you were doing there."

Beryl could hear what he said. She grabbed the phone, "Mr. Gerber. I apologize. The fault is mine. My name is Beryl Tilson. I'm writing an article about Piet Osterhaus for an American magazine. Gold mining in South America is of *enormous* interest. Jan is an old friend. I called him about my assignment and he mentioned his dad. He showed me the house which was so lovely and the gate was ajar. I apologize if our presence disturbed you or your family."

"What is the name of the publication you work for?" Gerber asked.

Beryl did not hesitate to answer. "Burnham Publications. Adventure Magazine, in Philadelphia." She gave him her office's 'spurious employment' number.

"I'll call you right back." He disconnected the call.

The phone rang in Wagner & Tilson's office and since the line had been set to answer with a voicemail message, he heard, "You've reached Adventure Magazine! The source of the seeker! If you know the extension of the party you wish to reach, please enter it now or press "1" to leave a message. If not, please press "0" and the next available consultant will answer your call." Those who pressed "0" would be treated to a local community college's rendition of Charles Ives' *Holidays Symphony - III. The Fourth of July.* Few callers waited.

Dolph Gerber realized his mistake and called again, pressing "1" to leave his phone number. Sensei Percy Wong returned his call. He checked various logs and then confirmed that Beryl Tilson was doing a story on The South American Gold Rush, featuring persons of interest.

While they waited for Dolph's return call, Jan poured another cup of coffee and pulled Beryl down onto his lap. *"Make me write bad checks,"* he said.

"The phone is likely to ring before you can find your check book."

The phone did ring again. Beryl answered. "I've just spoken to a fellow named Wong," Dolph said. "Do you know who that is?"

"My boss. I'm interested in anything about Piet Osterhaus. His adventures in gold prospecting... amusing or interesting anecdotes. If you have any of his old boots, scales, or crucibles, I'd like your permission to photograph them. Or any old non-copyrighted photos that have to do with mining - anything that our readers would enjoy. I have a deadline to keep, so if you're willing, I really would like to meet you."

"I'll see what I can find. Come by at one o'clock." He did not sound convinced.

"Thank you, Mr. Gerber. I'll see you at one."

.

For the rest of the morning, Beryl and Jan reviewed the old files. The crime scene photos were exactly what they would have expected if Greta Gerber had killed herself in such a peculiar way. The likely persons to have helped her were the persons who found her body; but since one of them, Andrea, was clearly supportive of Piet, that left Dolph as the likely accomplice.

While Jan waited outside, parked at the curb in his official Land Rover, Beryl knocked at the front door. Dolph Gerber answered and looked outside to see how and with whom she had arrived.

"That's Jan Osterhaus in his Land Rover," Beryl explained. "If it makes you uncomfortable to have it parked in front of your house, I'll go tell him to park in the next block to wait for me."

"No. It's not such a problem that it would warrant all that trouble."

"Any problem isn't worth it. One moment." She hurried back to Jan and asked him to move the car to a less noticeable area. Then she returned to Dolph Gerber. "See," she said as Jan started to pull away, "it was no trouble at all."

Gerber held the door open and she went inside.

He was a tall man, blue-eyed and of fair complexion. It struck Beryl as odd that he looked so much like Piet Osterhaus, whereas Piet's own son, Jan, did not look like his father at all. There was a quiet dignity about him, but it did not seem to be spontaneous. Every action he made, from the simplest gesture of indicating that she enter the living room to selecting the chair that he was going to sit on, was preceded by a thoughtful intention. There was a kind of time-delay, a half-second or so between his decision to act and the action. His eyes looked at the couch, and then he said, "Please sit down."

Across from the sofa were two upholstered chairs on either side of a lamp table. He looked at the chairs, first one and then the other, and decided to sit in one that was nearest a fireplace. Beryl wondered when they'd need a fireplace in the tropics.

He had piled odds and ends of mining gear onto the floor at the far end of the living room. He watched Beryl look around the quaintly furnished room. She suddenly had a peculiar expression of alarm on her face. "Are you looking for something?" he asked suspiciously.

"Light, for one thing. I'm trying to find the best place to take photographs. And the other thing is that Black Forest Cuckoo clock." She giggled nervously. "I'm not even going to tell you about me and my fear of Black Forest Cuckoo clocks."

Dolph Gerber laughed. "You've heard that they bring death."

"Yes! My mother refused to have one in the house. She was violent on the subject! Once a friend got one for her as a gift and sent it to the house and she wouldn't open it. A neighbor told her she was a suspicious fool. My mom said, 'Ok... if you like it so much, it's yours.' And I needn't tell you what happened next."

"Somebody died!"

"No, not somebody. Their cat was hit by a car. Which just goes to show you that cuckoo clocks kill."

Dolph laughed. "I've heard death stories from many people. I don't know how it became one of those urban legends or myths. People die after getting the cuckoo clock... maybe six years later–"

"Or a distant relative dies in another country!"

"Yes, and the poor clock is convicted. Ah, people need to make connections, I guess. Especially with clocks."

Beryl sat down and could not help but notice that she was surrounded by the eclectic choices of grandmothers everywhere. Wherever a human head might rest itself, there was a hand-crocheted doily: three on the sofa and one each on the upholstered chairs. She saw the Viennese drapes on the windows, the Hummel figurines, the 'shepherd and lady' porcelain figurines that formed the bases of several lamps, the needlepoint pillow coverings, and even the flowered wallpaper. The room was cluttered with knickknacks and elaborately framed photographs, magazine holders, ash trays, and empty candy dishes. The room said "Greta," and her son looked completely out of place sitting in it.

Dolph Gerber watched her take the room in as her glance swept it. "It's not what you'd call, 'a bachelor pad.'"

"Is this the way it was the day your mom died?"

"Yes."

"I understood that she played the piano. I don't see one."

"We have a soundproof music room upstairs."

"Ah... then she didn't perform for her guests."

"No, not in here, anyway. Sometimes when she was visiting a friend or neighbor who had a piano, she could be coaxed into playing. She liked Mozart."

"I'm puzzled. You're young... say, thirty-something, and you're single - or at least by my scanty research you're supposed to be—"

"I am thirty-three. And you're wondering why my 'availability status' isn't reflected in the room's decor."

"Well... yes. It's been over three years since your mom died. I'm assuming that you've kept it as she had kept it as some kind of *homage*."

"Then your assumption would be incorrect. I keep it like this because my little sister knows it like this. If I were to change it, she would be afraid to enter it."

"I see. Well, people get used to a certain kind of furniture and they don't want it changed. Not too long ago I read that after the War, Brazil decided to move its capital inland. I think they wanted to open up the vast interior. So they created Brasilia. Le Corbusier, the great French architect, was brought in to design the central buildings of the new city. It was all very modern, naturally. He designed one magnificent apartment building... lots of glass to let in the light... polished wood floors - the kind that could be set off with small area rugs of modernistic design. The decorated models of the various apartments were all furnished in exquisite Danish modern furniture - or something similar. And then people moved in. It's said that his heart was broken to see all the Chippendale and French Provincial and other indescribable styles being unloaded and carried into the place - and wall-to-wall shag carpeting, not to mention Viennese draped curtains covering his windows. He couldn't understand that a person's home and psyche tend to reflect each other; and if his psyche feels comfortable in a familiar Chippendale, that's what a person wants."

"So, in a sense, then, by leaving the room as it was - even for the sake of my kid sister - I'm reflecting my mother's 'psyche' as you put it."

Beryl shrugged. "Or not..."

"Not! I dislike Black Forest Cuckoo clocks. I can hear the damned thing all the way up in my bedroom. It doesn't know how to shut up during nighttime hours."

"How can it stop? People are dying all over the world!" She laughed and he joined in. They giggled about the clock and the formality crumbled. It was a fortuitous beginning. Beryl liked the man and had the feeling that he liked her as well. "Tell me about Piet Osterhaus. I don't want his private life. But rather, how often did he go mining? Was your mom worried that something would happen to him when he went? Did he come home and tell you stories about an anaconda that tried to swallow his shovel? Or acquaintances who turned out to be claim jumpers. Things like that."

"He went once a month and usually stayed at least a week. He kept the location of the site a secret. He never registered the claims. You understand that to do so would have invited scores of prospectors to the sites. When I traced the maps he left, only one site was available for examination. There were four total, and three were on lands ceded to Indian tribes or leased to commercial lumber interests. The one I did manage to see was down in Sipaliwini near the Kutari River... actually near the point that Brazil, Guyana, and Suriname meet. There was a lot of old rusted-out mining stuff there. But someone must have found the site and had used it as a campsite or dwelling of some kind. I saw many of his old pans and shovels, but the place gave me the creeps. Crocodiles the size of motor canoes. Snakes that looked to be a foot in diameter and twenty meters long... of course, I'm exaggerating. I'm a city person. I call the exterminator if I see an unusual spider in the house.

"My mother worried about him. It would have been naive to imagine that he wasn't in danger. Once he did fall and got a gash in his head. He was tough. He walked the few miles through the bush to where he hid his motorcycle... he had off-road tires on it. And he managed to drive the cycle all the way back to Kwamalasamutu where he kept his single engine plane. He had thirteen stitches put in his head when he got home here in Paramaribo. You'd need a plane and a motorcycle to get to his mining site, and then you'd have to go a few miles on foot, and also cross a river."

"I'm intrigued. I'd love to see it. Could a helicopter get a person near the site? You know, hover over it and let you down a ladder or basket?"

Dolph put his head back and laughed heartedly. "Would you go through the expense of hiring a helicopter just for a few photographs?"

Beryl looked at the pile of miner's gear on the floor. "All right. For a two page story, no. But this was an extraordinary man, a complicated one. A secret map! That's got the allure of a treasure map. Did he leave any journals? Did he run into any hostile Indians? And old photos! Lord, I would kill for a few old photos of him at the placer site. The Golden Fleece! Do you know the story of the Golden Fleece?"

"Jason and the Argonauts? What does that have to do with Piet?"

"Placer miners used the fleece of a sheep to catch the flecks of gold as the muddy sluice water flowed over it. It worked like riffles in a sluice box. The fleece would get heavy with gold. It became a treasure... all by itself."

"Ah. I didn't know that. He had some kind of sluice there. I didn't see any fleece, but unless it happened to be tanned, the animals would have eaten it, with or without gold." He pointed to the pile of old mining artifacts. "Take a look at this stuff. I'll make us some tea or would you prefer coffee?"

"Tea."

Dolph left the room. Beryl went to the pile and knelt down to examine some of the items - a tool belt that had masonry chisels and a miner's pick, several pans, and a canteen. She picked up the canteen and heard something move inside it. She shook it and, certain that there was something in it, she unscrewed the lid and turned the canteen upside down. She shook it until a rolled up piece of paper fell out. She opened the paper and saw a hand-drawn map. "Dolph!" she called. "Come look at this!"

Gerber came into the living room, carrying a tray that contained a tea pot and cups. He saw her holding out the paper and the canteen. She wasn't trying to memorize its features. It was written in Dutch and she couldn't understand it, anyway.

He looked over her shoulder. "That's the map of the one place I could find," he said, setting the tray down. "I followed it. Don't tell me you want to go all the way down there."

"Why not? If I get out of line you can feed me to one of those crocodiles."

"Can you afford to rent a helicopter?"

"Ahhh. That depends on what it costs. What are we talking about? How much does it cost to rent a helicopter for a day? Or, can I take a cheap commercial flight down there and rent a motorcycle for the day?"

"You'd never find it."

"So, along with the plane and the motorcycle, I'd have to rent you for the day. Are you expensive?"

"Very. But not for you. I like that you didn't try to steal the map. Most people would have. There are also innocent people who were badly hurt by Piet's trial and conviction, and in some small way, a nice article about him that emphasized his normal life, would help to take that onus off them."

"Does this mean you'll be my guide to his former mine/squatter's campsite?"

"Be here at 8 a.m. tomorrow morning. We'll ride one of Piet's Harleys to the heliport. I keep a dirt bike in the hangar. We'll load that one onto the chopper; and then we'll head southwest, making stops at Pokigron, Peleloetepu, and then Kwamalasamutu. I need to take the 'copter on a shake-out run." He pointed on the map to the last place he had named. It was written in a scrawled hand. From that town, there was a road-line drawn in a southwest direction. He pointed to the road. "That's actually a trail... single file but a cycle can handle it. Then we leave the cycle here..." He pointed to a circled X on the map. "And from there walk in. There's a creek we have to cross. If it's raining, it becomes a river. So all in all we have to go on foot a few kilometers - a couple of miles, more or less. We can take photos and come back to where we left the cycle and then ride back to where the helicopter is waiting."

"All these stops you've indicated... are they tiny outposts... just refueling stations... or are there people living there?"

"They're all not the same size. I started to go down a second time and took the Piper. But it started to rain and I decided not to go past Peleloetepu. 'Outpost' is a good way to describe these places. Refueling stations. The mining companies need them. Fuel is expensive; but what else can they do? There's usually a little restaurant and depending on the local inhabitants, the food varies from ok to not so good."

"All right then... how about filling that canteen with fresh water and I'll stop at a sporting goods' shop and get boots and a machete and some freeze dried food rations and meet you here at 8 a.m. Do I call anyone to hire the helicopter?"

"No. I'll take you there. Piet owned a helicopter service. My sister and I inherited it."

Beryl noted that he used the singular "sister." "Where is your sister now? In school?"

"No. I have two sisters, actually. Andrea is married and living in Aruba. She's out of the picture, so to speak. I keep her photograph." He nodded at a table that contained several framed photos. "My other sister is my kid sister, Juliana. She's having a surgical procedure done in Brazil. She should be back on Friday. That's why I'm rushing the time to go to the campsite. And, naturally," he joked, "I must do all that I can to accommodate your deadline."

"Well, I'm sorry to have missed them."

"You won't be mentioning them in your article?"

"Not unless they have a mining story they want to tell."

"They won't. Your tea..."

Beryl took the cup of tea. "I was going to say, 'I'll pass on the tea,' but frankly, this smells too good. What is it?"

"Darjeeling. My mother's favorite."

34

"It's delicious. She had nice taste."

.

Jan said, "No" a half-dozen times in rapid succession. "No, no, no, no, no, and No! *Nein! Niet!* No Way. Have you any idea what you'll encounter down there? No! Of course you don't. If you did you never would have come up with this hare brained scheme."

"I don't have any Kevlar-lined pants this trip. I'll have to get high boots. And some good knives."

"No."

"Take me to a place where I can buy boots."

"No. I'm not going to let you risk your life just to make my step-mother - or whatever the hell Helena is to me - happy. I don't give a shit if my old man becomes the next Dracula. What do you hope to learn down there anyway?"

"I've never had an Adolph make love to me. I don't want to be eaten by a crocodile or swallowed whole by an anaconda until I've checked-off all the items on my 'bucket list.'"

Jan pulled into a parking place and turned off the engine. "You are the reason men turn to domestic violence... because women like you drive them crazy."

"I resent that. Dolphie told me I was unique, but you say I'm just like every other woman who gets eaten by a crocodile." She did not realize that she had underestimated his concern.

Jan clutched the wheel and leaned forward until his forehead touched it. He spoke softly. "Is this what life with you must always be like? One dangerous situation after another. I sit and wait wondering, scared about what is waiting out there to hurt you, fearing the worst the entire time you're gone. Is this what being with you is always going to be?"

"Honey," she said, joking, "you're no different from any cop's wife. It's my job. It's a dirty job but somebody's gotta do it."

Before she finished the sentence he had begun to laugh. "Kill me now!" he said, starting the car again.

"Jan, dear... Dolph is our prime suspect in being his mother's accomplice. Somebody took that gun away. Somebody moved that board away and stood it against the shed. I've told him I'm writing a story about Piet Osterhaus's mining operations. How can I reasonably fail to be interested in his mining site? None of this family saga makes the slightest bit of sense. You called me down here because Helena is pestering you to investigate her husband's affairs. And this is precisely what I'm doing."

.

The boots he selected came up to mid thigh and then the tops folded down to nearly the knee. She put them on and looked in the mirror. "I look like Puss'n'Boots."

Jan could not stop laughing and had to leave the shop. Before the door closed he hollered, "She'll take them!"

Beryl waited until he returned. "Seriously," she said, "I look like I'm playing a duke in some Restoration Comedy. All I need is a blue sash and a big hat with ostrich plumes."

Jan laughed even harder. His eyes were filled with tears and he had to catch his breath repeatedly. "She also wants a machete that she can slip through her blue sash." He finally controlled his laughter enough to ask, "Can you also give her a hunter's 'Dayglo' orange hat and vest?" He handed the clerk his credit card.

.

On their way back to his apartment, he stopped at his office to make arrangements for a government helicopter to take him and an off-road motorcycle down to Kwamalasamutu and to pick up a satellite phone for Beryl. "I'll be there before you arrive," he said. "Tell Dolphie to watch his step when he's around my woman. I'm probably a better shot than he is."

"I think I told you that the trail we take sort of heads southwest towards the Guyana and Brazilian border. And we have to cross a river."

"A lot of that area is disputed territory. Suriname claims it but the Guyanese government insists that it belongs to them. Because of its questioned ownership, there is little law enforcement there. You will not be in safe territory. It is a haven for fugitives. I want you to wear the orange hat and vest since I'll be following you. I can't get too close without him thinking that I'm a claim-jumper or a man out to steal a woman. Do you understand what I'm telling you?"

"Yes... I know what to expect. The worst. I'm glad you'll be there."

Jan made a series of phone calls and set the alarm for 5:30 a.m. "Tomorrow morning, we'll have breakfast. For the record, you never know what kind of weather you'll run into in March. I'll give you a can of insect repellent. Use it. Keep the insects off you. The stuff stinks but it also has the effect of making you taste awful to leeches and wasps and bot flies and mosquitos. Jesus... I need my head examined. All right. We'll eat and get ready and I'll take you to Dolph's house and drop you off outside at 7:45 a.m. I'll go on to the airport immediately and be flying down ahead of you. I'll be in a faster chopper than anything he's got in his little fleet. I'll be waiting for you down by the airstrip.

"Here! I got you a satellite phone. You have my number. If you get stuck anyplace, just call me. I can get the call even if I'm airborne. Are we set?"

"No. How can I explain the appearance of a government satellite phone when I'm just a poor little free lance journalist? I do not want a satellite phone!"

"I know that you know enough to know that the jungle is a dangerous place. How can you reject a piece of equipment like this?"

Beryl shook her head. "I don't expect the kind of trouble that a phone call would solve. You know, 'Hello Jan. *The anaconda is wrapping itself around me. Should I hang up and call 9-1-1?*' ... or maybe, '*Hi Jan, the crocodile has me in its jaws and I can't read the GPS coordinates to tell you where I'm being consumed.*' Or maybe--" Jan put his hand over her mouth and lifted her off the ground.

"Let's go out and get some of that fruit salad again. You can't talk while you're eating."

"All right. We need to get back and get to sleep. Big big day tomorrow. *Oh Jan! I'm being eaten by Piranha! How soon can you get here?*"

THURSDAY, MARCH 22, 2012

It had rained through the night, just a shower that left beads of water on the patio table and fused together the clusters of mimosa flowers that drooped from the trees. If there had been any city dust in Paramaribo's air, it now had been washed into the culverts and gullies. It was still too early to distinguish individual clouds in the overhead mist of dawn; but if the sun did elect to shine on that Thursday morning, it would meet no impediment.

Jan slipped out of bed at the first hint of eastern light, knowing that it was still too early to guess whether the day would be cloudy or clear. He turned off the bedside alarm clock. There was no need for it now as he went out onto the patio. Birds chirped, chattered, and sang in the symphonia trees and palms, and many swooped down to fish for earthworms that lay on the edges of puddles. March weather was capricious and being so, was dangerous to creatures that were unprepared for change.

Jan swiped his hand across the table top, sending splashes of water off the table edge. Careful to make no disturbance, he came inside and closed the bedroom door, carried out a bath towel to dry the table top and chairs, and then brought to the patio the noisy coffee grinder and a supply of hazelnut flavored beans that Beryl liked. He ground the beans and returned to the kitchen to fill the coffee maker with water and the powdered beans. She would want fresh fruit, yogurt and granola. He brought the food to the table, covering it with a screened dome. The sky was different now. He could see red edges to the grey shapes that were passing overhead, but in the East, there was only blue and gold. He heard the pipes clang and knew that Beryl was in the shower. He finished

38

setting the table and sat down to wait for a beautiful day that seemed inexplicably filled with dread.

Jan stopped outside the Gerber house and waited to see the front door open and Beryl enter the building. He continued on to the next block, parked, and waited until he saw her and Dolph drive past on the Harley. Knowing that their destination was a private heliport near Zorg En Hoop airport, he drove on to the government section of the airport. The military helicopter was ready to go.

Dolph parked in his company hangar and walked out an off-road motorcycle which he parked beside the helicopter they would be using: a new McDonnell Douglas 500E. The sight of the aircraft gave her the assurance that she would be in a fast reliable vehicle, and took away the assurance that Jan's bigger lumbering government helicopter would arrive in Kwamalasamutu ahead of her and Dolph. This was worrisome. She planned to stall as much as possible during their stops on the way south.

An attendant helped to load the motorcycle into the fuselage of the helicopter. The attendant did not tell anyone that an hour earlier, a government agent had put a GPS indicator under the seat of the motorcycle and told him not to disclose this to anyone.

Beryl and Dolph climbed into the McDonnell Douglas; and to her surprise, Dolph took the controls. "For some reason," she said, "I thought we'd have a pilot."

"You do. Me. If you want to go from point A to point B, you need to know how to fly, even if it's to relieve your pilot in case he passes out."

"Ah," Beryl said. "I hope you are in good health."

"To be honest, rather than pilot failure, it's engine failure you'd have to worry about; and then it wouldn't help you if you did know how to fly. A helicopter is not a glider. We'd go down and usually what's beneath us is either treetops or water. No matter how much finesse you bring to your landing, you're gonna get mangled in the trees or if you should land in water, the jaws of a caiman.

"Soon," he announced, "we'll be flying over the Sipaliwini District, the largest state in Suriname. In fact, it's about half the size of the country - the southern rainforest half."

"What's this aircraft's range?" Beryl asked.

"Don't worry about range. Suriname is about the size of the state of Georgia. I haven't flown this chopper any distance. This, technically, is its shake-out flight. With a range in excess of 300 miles, I don't think we have too much to worry about. Electrical storms are another story. I'll make a couple of stops just so you can get the feel of the people who inhabit isolated areas in the electronic age."

They touched down at Pokigron, a village on the red clay banks of the Brokopondo Reservoir. Beryl took a few photos of Adolph and the natives as the helicopter was getting fuel. "We can go much farther," Dolph explained, "but sometimes it is better to have more fuel than we need than..." he smiled and she finished his sentence, "to have less than we need."

Airborne again, they continued southwest heading for Peleloetepu. The land became a vast green blanket. "There's a place in Guatemala," she said, "on the continental divide. A mountain range called the Cuchumatanes divides the country in half. The northern side of the mountains gets the weather of the Caribbean or Atlantic side, and the southern side of the mountains gets the drier Pacific weather. There's a town on the northern foothills called *Ilom* which means 'The View.' And in the morning when you look in front of you there is the Ixcan section of the Peten rain forest below - an immense wall-to-wall carpet of treetops. The morning mist lies over the trees like a layer of cotton candy and then the morning sun just dissolves it in its light... like your tongue laps up cotton candy. This must look just like that in the morning."

"It does. And it is an addictive sight to see."

A large section of land had been cleared in Peleloetepu and Dolph landed the chopper smoothly. Ordinary winged aircraft were landing on the airstrip, their touchdown and trip to the gate obviously bumpy for them. Dolph bought a few Cokes and they were on their way again.

The helicopter's pulsing hum became as monotonous as the landscape beneath. "It's like being on a train when there's another train on the track beside you," Dolph said. "When there's movement of one of them, you can't tell which one. Up here, with the endless green world underneath, it sometimes feels that you're still and the world is passing beneath you."

They continued westward until they approached Kwamalasamutu and landed gracefully compared to a winged aircraft that had just touched-down and was bouncing along the dirt runway. There were many more huts, and at first Beryl had difficulty orienting herself since the sun was overhead. She searched for a government helicopter and found none although there was an area of the field that she couldn't clearly see. There were several winged aircraft at the side of the little hangar.

The natives who approached the helicopter thought at first that they were conservationists, but Dolph, speaking in a dialect Beryl did not recognize, told them that they were simple tourists who wanted to take a ride through the bush on an all-terrain vehicle. People shrugged and offered a few items for sale... mostly foodstuffs and canned beverages... and the motorcycle was unloaded and fueled.

Jan stood in the shadows at the far side of the field and watched them. He had arrived an hour ahead of them and had begun to worry. His motorcycle was ready to go. He watched them leave on Dolph's cycle, and then, making sure that his GPS tracker was on, he began to follow.

Beryl, sporting her orange hat and vest over a long sleeved cotton shirt and boot-cut blue jeans over her "Puss'n'Boots" high tops, sat behind Dolph on the motorcycle. In a few minutes they were at the southern edge of the thatched hut village and disappeared into the bush.

At a place indicated on the crude map by a circled X, they parked the cycle. Jan, who had watched their movement closely on the GPS indicator, saw that they had stopped moving and cut his engine. He began to walk his cycle down the narrow trail until finally he saw the place where Dolph and Beryl had cut foliage to drape over their parked cycle.

Jan had no idea how far in front of him they were. Now and then he thought he saw a glimpse of orange, but he could never be sure. Parrots and other colorful birds and blooming trees easily deceived the eye. He told himself that there simply could not be that many trails for anyone to take and that if he followed the one he was on, he was bound to reach his father's camp.

Their trail, he saw to his dismay, left little indication that it had been trod upon. The leaves were damp, thickly piled, and spongy. They did not break when they were compressed by a footstep and quickly rebounded to their previous thickness. An expert could possibly have tracked them, Jan decided, but he was not an expert. Beryl and Dolph came to a broad section of river that they were able to cross by a series of stepping stones. Jan watched them cross and then he carefully followed. The river was low. He estimated that if it flowed even six inches higher, it would not have been possible to cross on foot. Jan looked at the sky and noted with concern that it was cloudy.

Ahead, at the camp, a renegade Indian nicknamed "Prego," cooked a fish through which he had rammed a spit. He slowly rotated the large fish over the fire. The odor of the roasting fish reached Dolph and Beryl. "Someone's at the camp," Dolph said.

"Maybe it's the same person who was living here the last time you came."

Dolph immediately became cautious. He had suspected that they were being followed a few miles back. He had also heard Jan's motorcycle continue to run after he had turned off the ignition of his own cycle. He wondered if this trip were some kind of set-up. Confronting her, he asked, "Is that camper up ahead a friend of yours?"

"No," she said. "I have no idea who that could be. But I hope he's not an enemy, either. This place does give a person the creeps."

"What about the person who's following us? Do you know who it is?"

"If I'm not mistaken, it's Jan. He made me wear this orange hat and vest. He's not interested in the mining site. He's just worried about me."

"You're not really a journalist, are you?"

"No. I'm a private investigator. Helena Osterhaus is driving Jan crazy about clearing her husband's name. She wanted him to call in a P.I. and since Jan couldn't care less about his father... apparently they detested each other... he thought he'd kill two birds with one stone. We were an 'item' a year or so ago."

"Yes. I thought the name 'Wong' sounded familiar. He was on TV having something to do with Japanese knives. There was a great picture of you in the Sunday paper."

"Get Out! We went home on Saturday. Jan never told me that there were published pictures of us taken... Where? At the Japanese Embassy party?"

"Yes. You were wearing a dark colored sari."

"Sensei Percy Wong bought that for me in Paramaribo. I must see if the newspaper has that shot available for me. I'd like a copy."

They passed stony outcrops that grew taller and more impassible. Soon they were walking on a path that had a cliff on one side and the river on the other. "We've got only one way to run," she said. "And that's to retreat."

"And then we'll run right into Jan who I hope is armed."

Ahead, Prego looked down at them from a ledge. "A friend of yours, I hope," she said, joking.

"Sorry," Dolph said. "I have no friends down here." He smiled and called to the man, "Hello!"

The man watched them approach as they parted the brush at the edge of the clearing. He held a rifle. "Ovah he'ah," he said.

Beryl stared at him incredulously. His appearance was frightening in a grotesque comic book way. He had suffered from a scalp condition... most of his hair was missing. Clumps of it grew normally, but the scalp between the clumps of hair was gnarled and scarred with strange caterpillar sized bumps. She had seen television shows about parasites and wondered if these bumps were large bot fly maggots under his skin. His nose had been broken and allowed to heal pushed to one side. His teeth were missing in front: all the incisors, both upper and lower, were gone; and the rest of his teeth were black and rotten. His body was tattooed with 'prison tats' - artless insignia of organizations, mottos, demonic heroes, and totem animals - and it was also covered in sores and scabs.

"Hello," Dolph called, concealing his revulsion and trying to seem harmless and friendly. "We smelled your fish cooking. This is a nice place you've got here."

Beryl looked around. The river nearby was no doubt filled with piranha, crocodile, and possibly electric eels. Its banks had to be occupied - to some degree or other - by anaconda and other constrictors, numerous poisonous reptiles, and lethal-to-the-touch amphibians. She refused to think about spiders.

Dolph looked up at the man on the ledge. "I'm Dolph and this lady is Beryl. We're just tourists."

"Prego," the man said. "Tha's ma name. Prego." He climbed down a ladder and looked at Beryl as though she were sliced into cutlets on a tray in a butcher's window. He went to the cooking fire and rotated the spit.

She looked up at the ledge. "No doubt," she thought, "that is where he sleeps. If he brings the ladder up with him, not even a monkey could get up there." She also saw numerous gasoline cans. It made no sense to have so much gasoline for a motorcycle. There had to be other machinery. "Is this a mining claim?" she innocently asked.

"It use'ta be," Prego said. "Gold's all gone now."

Dolph came to Beryl's side. He whispered, "I've heard his name before. Who is this guy?" To Prego he said, "This is a nice hideaway. Everything you need. Fish… snake… probably a lot of birds' eggs."

"Ahm Prego," the man repeated. "Ya hearda' me?"

Dolph smiled. "I haven't heard of anyone. We're new to the area, Mr. Prego."

"May we sit and join you?" Beryl said sweetly. "It's hot and we've walked a few miles through the bush." Since she heard no objection she found a clear place on the ground some forty feet from where Prego stood. She sat down, appearing to be relaxed.

"Got any water to drink?" Dolph asked, just to have something non-threatening to say.

"Tha' can the'ah. Go down and get ya'self a drink."

Beryl did not know whether or not Dolph was aware of a crocodile's peculiar habit of lying submerged, very close to the water's edge, so that the slightest disturbance of the water's surface would cause it to leap up and grab in its great jaws any creature that was foolish enough to disturb the surface. "Take a stick," she called, "and poke the area at the edge in case there's a croc waiting under the surface to bite you."

Dolph already had a stick in his hand. He understood the habits of crocodiles. But Prego blamed Beryl for spoiling "the little joke." "Why' ju haf ta tell him?" he said, pointing the rifle at her. "You'z a wildcat."

"I didn't tell him. He already knew."

Dolph returned with water that he did not intend to drink. "Want some?" he asked Prego.

"Lemme see ya' wallet!" Prego demanded, pointing the rifle at him.

Dolph obliged, assuming that the man did not know how to read. "I don't have much money."

"Ya he'ah to jump ma claim?" Prego asked.

"No," Dolph answered defensively. "Would I bring a woman with me to jump a claim... not that I would jump anybody's claim if I were alone."

"Ya' lyin'" he shouted. Then he looked over at Beryl. "She ya' wife?" Prego asked, pointing the rifle at Beryl.

"No, she's just a friend of the family."

"How'dja get he'ah? Gotta motah cycle stowed back the'ah. Ah heard it befo' ya got he'ah." He took the wallet and pointed the rifle at Dolph as he looked through its contents. He pulled various credit cards out of their slots and ominously tossed them to the ground. He removed the money and tossed the wallet behind him.

"Gimme tha keys to tha' motah cycle. Gimme 'em now."

Dolph looked over at Beryl. "We have to get going now," he said. "It's getting late."

"Gimme tha' keys!" He turned to Beryl. "Toss that machet' ovah he'ah. Do it now o' ah just might kill this fella!" She unbuckled the belt that held the machete's scabbard and tossed it towards him.

Dolph reached into his pocket and pulled out the ignition key. "Here," he said, handing the key to Prego who took it and fired a single shot into Dolph's thigh. Immediately, Dolph fell to the ground, wincing in pain and bleeding profusely.

Beryl jumped up, but he pointed the rifle at her. "Get yo ass up that laddah! Now!" He pulled the rifle's lever down, putting in place another bullet. He had already demonstrated his willingness to kill and he was too far away from her to consider hand-to-hand combat. "Move!" he shouted.

Beryl went to the ladder and began to climb it. After she had gone about six rungs up, she could see over the top into the cave-like ledge. There was a generator at one end and wires that led from it and crossed to the middle of the grotto-like ledge where a DVD monitor and other electronic equipment were positioned. On the other side of the ledge was a mattress and bolster, positioned so that he could sit up and watch the monitor. There was a stack of DVDs, none of which seemed to be in a professional case. She also saw a box of women's jewelry sitting open on the floor. Some of the jewelry looked expensive. There was a small pile of women's clothing in one corner.

While Dolph writhed on the ground, Prego slung his rifle over his shoulder and grabbed the ladder at the base. He had one foot on the bottom rung and the other foot extended to step on the next rung when a shot rang out and he toppled back, nearly pulling the ladder with him. Jan appeared at the edge of the clearing.

"Dolph's been shot!" Beryl shouted as she slid down the ladder and checked to see that Prego was dead. She picked up his rifle.

Jan got on the satellite phone and called for his helicopter. "There's not much area to land in and the man cannot be carried," he said. "Tree overhang?" he asked, and signaled Beryl to check the open area of the river.

Beryl ran to the river's edge. She called back, "There are big stones in the middle of the river up ahead. The river is much wider there. If the chopper can lower a basket down to the middle where those stones are, we can get Dolph out there."

Jan asked them to fly over and to judge if it would be safe for them to maneuver in a tight environment. "We'll get the patient out to the rocks." He paused to listen to a question. "Yes," he answered. "The patient is the man who flew that MD 500 down here. It's his aircraft."

Jan, looking for something to carry Dolph in, found an old string hammock. "This will have to do," he said, spreading it on the ground beside Dolph. Beryl lay the rifle down and helped Jan to lift Dolph onto the hammock. They could hear the chopper approach.

Beryl took the belt which held the machete scabbard and used it as a tourniquet on Dolph's thigh. "I don't think the bullet hit your femoral artery, but it tapped into something big. You're really bleeding."

"Look," Jan said. "It's too dangerous - from several aspects - to attempt to cross to those rocks with a bleeding man. You just help me get him to the river's edge and then cover me as I try to cross. Here's my Colt, and use that rifle if you need to."

"Help is on the way," Beryl told Dolph who continued to grimace and groan in pain. She picked up one end of the hammock and hoisted it onto her shoulder. Jan took the other end and they slowly went a few meters below the rocks to compensate for the force of the current. "With him so bloody, there's no way we can get him over to the rocks. We'll have to bring the basket to shore." They set the hammock down and Jan went a few meters above the rocks, also to compensate for the current's force as he swam to the rocks.

The noise and wind generated by the aircraft prevented them from hearing anything. They responded only to what they could see. A soldier leaned out of the chopper's side and then, from a mechanism, a rope that secured a man-sized basket was lowered.

Trees overhung the side of the river on which Dolph lay. Jan reached the rocks and looked at the rushing water. He stripped off his shirt and gestured that he'd tow the basket over to the shore. He tied one sleeve-end around the edge of the basket and the other around his belt and plunged into the river, fighting the current as he tried to drag the basket to the tree lined shore. As the water pushed him in an angle that carried him below the place where Beryl waited, she moved with him along the shore.

The man in the chopper played out an excess of line so that Jan could reach the riverbank without the line being snared by the treetops. At that point he and Beryl could then grab the basket and drag it back along the bank to where Dolph was lying in the hammock.

As they moved along the riverbank, Beryl could not hear a caiman make a hissing noise as it skidded through the mud; but her eye did catch its movement. She took Jan's Colt from her belt and fired twice at the caiman. The animal merely turned and went into the water. They reached Dolph and loaded him into the basket. When he was securely strapped in, Beryl dove into the water and guided the basket out from under the overhanging branches. The man in the helicopter suddenly stood in the opening with a rifle. She saw but did not hear the shot. When she looked back at where he seemed to be pointing, she could see the upturned head of the caiman she had tried to kill. She looked up at the soldier and made a thumb's up sign and continued to pull as Jan pushed the basket clear of the trees.

The basket began to be reeled in, but because of the turbulence, it began to swing back and forth like an errant pendulum.

Jan took Beryl's hand and pulled her through the sucking mud up onto the riverbank. He put his shirt on and picked up the rifle and gun she had left at the river's edge. Together they watched the basket swing back and forth, skimming the river until the copter rose, then skimming the tree tops as the copter climbed. Finally the basket was taken into the aircraft. The soldier gave a salute to Jan, and the helicopter rose up and away, quickly out of view.

"Well," said Jan, "that was a strange and mysterious event. At least, I thought it was. How about you?"

"I've had less exciting moments," Beryl said. The two of them walked over to Prego.

"What the hell happened to this guy?" Jan said. "Did you catch his name?"

"Prego. I know it means 'please' in Italian. But that's what he said his name is."

"Jesus," said Jan. "I know who this guy is. He's wanted in several countries... for murder, among other things. What was he doing in my father's camp?"

"He lives up on the ledge," she said. "There's a small cave up there. He's got a generator and a DVD player."

"What?"

"He's got a generator, a DVD monitor and equipment, a stack of home-made DVDs, a bed and all kinds of women's junk up there. Take a look for yourself!"

Beryl climbed the ladder and stepped onto the ledge. Jan followed. "Look at all this jewelry," she said. "Some of it looks valuable." She rummaged through the box. "There's a couple of wedding rings here... and wrist watches." She looked up with a fearful expression, "I wonder what happened to the women who wore them?"

Jan opened a box that was filled with blank DVD disks. "Does that equipment burn DVDs as well as play them?" Jan asked, stooping down to look at the controls. "Damn," he said. "They can copy DVDs here. What did they do here? Pirate movies? Porn?" He picked up a stack of home made movies. Let's take them and get the hell out of here."

Beryl was more interested in the jewelry. "This jewelry may belong to women who've been missing. Your missing-persons people need to check these items." She got a shirt from the pile of garments and put the box of jewelry into the shirt and pushed it down into her tote bag. Jan put the used DVDs into a shirt and tied it securely to the back of his gun belt. "Can you drive a motorcycle?"

"I haven't driven one in a long time... but I think I can manage."

They left Prego's body where it lay. He appeared to be too diseased to risk touching. Beryl thoroughly photographed him with her iPhone. "Let's just cover him with rocks," she suggested. It seemed like the best of all possible solutions.

They covered his body with stones and then picked up Dolph's wallet, credit cards, and the motorcycle key that were lying on the ground. "Did he touch them?" Jan asked.

"Yes, for a moment before he shot Dolph."

Jan picked up the key. "We're gonna need a very good bath."

Beryl looked at the site. "We touched the ladder," she reminded him, "and the rifle."

Dolph Gerber's helicopter was still parked beside the hangar. "Can you pilot this thing?" Beryl asked.

"This is state of the art. I can fly smaller, older models, but I won't risk trying to operate this baby." He asked the hangar manager, "Anybody around who can handle this?"

"What about him?" the manager pointed to a uniformed man who was jogging across the field towards them.

"He was on board with us when I came down," Jan noted.

The soldier saluted as he approached. "Sir, before the captain headed for the hospital he said to tell you that while he appreciated your many talents he thought this fine machine would be better off in my hands."

Jan looked at the clean interior of the chopper. "We might as well leave the cycles here. We'll be back soon enough." He turned to the hangar manager. "Is it ok to leave the bikes here in your office? We'll be back within 48 hours."

"Sure," the manager said. "Wait... here are some old newspapers to put on the seat."

"Gotta bag?" Jan asked.

The manager returned with a large plastic bag. Jan stripped off his wet uniform, shoes and socks, and put them in the bag. Beryl tossed her orange hat and vest into the bag and let him pull her "Puss'n'Boots " footwear off and add them to the bag's contents. Then she lined the seat with some of the newspapers and gave the rest to Jan who spread them on the floor of the fuselage. Shoeless and in his underwear, Jan sat down and said, "Ok, Lieutenant. We're set to go."

The flight back to Paramaribo had a post-climactic dreariness about it. For half an hour, neither of them spoke. Jan finally asked, "I wonder if my father knew that guy?"

"Probably. When Dolph heard the name, he seemed to remember it. It's not the sort of name a person's likely to forget."

Nothing further was said. Jan remained deep in thought about his father, the peculiar campsite, women's jewelry and garments, and the man who inhabited the site.

As soon as they landed in Paramaribo, the pilot went into the hangar and returned with an old pair of pants and a shirt for Jan to put on before he talked to a group of waiting officers. He assured everyone that he would be making an immediate report from his office.

Jan called the hospital and learned that Dolph was still in surgery. "At least he made it into the O.R.," he told Beryl.

They drove to his apartment, pulled off their clothing, put all of their garments in the washing machine, added soap powder and more than enough bleach, and then got into the tub-shower and began to scrub themselves. There was no mirth, no joking, no smiles or pleasantries. Everything was grim and silent.

They both put on fresh clothing and latex gloves. "Let us see what this mystery is all about," said Jan, as he put the first DVD into the player.

Less than a minute into the video he suddenly realized what he was looking at and he gasped and got up and went into the bathroom and retched. Beryl turned down the volume and stayed to watch the actions of people she did not know. A Viking type of man, whom Beryl recognized from the various photographs Jan had sent her, appeared usually wearing a devil's mask. He was performing abominable sexual acts upon a girl of approximately thirteen who was screaming in pain and crying. The room appeared to be of the same style as the Gerber house. Beryl watched the entire video and then went to Jan's desk and got a black felt pen. "P with 13 year old girl," she titled the disk. She put the next one into the slot. This was of the same girl who perhaps was a year younger. She could hardly believe what the man was forcing her to do. She kept the volume as low as possible. The man was speaking Dutch and it seemed to Beryl that whenever the girl started to cry, the man would whip her feet and insist that she smile and tell him she wanted him to do more of what had made her cry. He had a variety of instruments, and he used them on all of her most tender areas, pinching and twisting.

"Thank God I had a son," she said aloud. She tagged this one, "P with 12 year old girl."

After watching the tapes for three hours, Beryl went out to the patio. "Why don't you walk down to that pizza place and get us something to eat."

Jan came into the room and, without looking at the screen, said, "How much longer do you think this will take, totally?"

"I have three DVDs left; but I don't know how much of each is used. It could be an hour or three hours. When you get back I'd like to take another shower. If you pass a store that sells women's clothing, get me more jeans and shirts… size 8 or 10. And buy more bleach."

Three videos that were recorded in the cave-ledge were of Prego and women who had come to the site expecting to be well paid for their services that they had assumed would be used by Piet. All three women had identical reactions when they saw Prego hand the camera to Piet. As each saw Prego coming towards her, she screamed and tried to climb down the ladder. In all three cases, Prego grabbed the woman's hair, pulled her back into the cave, tied her wrists behind her, gagged her, and proceeded to torture her sexually. The torture continued until the DVD ended either by having reached its capacity or by the woman falling dead or unconscious.

As far as Beryl could tell, the videos of Piet recorded the torment of only one girl who was probably Juliana. Evidently, Piet had the presence of mind to torment only one of the sisters. The other would then, of course, be able to testify that he was the very model of a wonderful stepfather. The abuse had been recorded from the time the girl was a toddler.

Jan returned before Beryl had finished watching the last video. He went back to the patio table and sat motionless, waiting for her. The late afternoon sun was in his face, but he did not blink or close his eyes. She saw a bag of clothing that he had laid on the bed. She went into the bathroom and again took another shower, toweled off, and put the new garments on. Then she went to him and shook his shoulder gently. "I've seen them all. You can come in now."

Jan followed her inside. "Were they all the same?"

"Worse. Same girl. From the age of three until about thirteen."

"What am I going to do?"

"I labeled the disks and boxes and put them all in a paper shopping bag I found. I put the bag behind the couch. You don't ever want to see them."

"What should I do with them?" Jan continued to be dazed and uncomprehending.

"First, you need to put the jewelry and the shirts into an evidence bag. That jewelry may belong to women who've disappeared. Their families may be looking for them. For now let's just eat and watch some TV and go to bed. Tomorrow we can talk about it. Today nothing can possibly make sense."

Jan had been calling the hospital, getting hourly reports on "my stepbrother Dolph Gerber's condition." The reports were all encouraging. Jan said that he'd check again in the morning.

They ate pizza and tried to concentrate on the TV screen; but the effort failed. Finally, Jan went to his medicine cabinet and brought two tranquilizers into the living room. They washed them down with the last of their Cokes.

FRIDAY, MARCH 23, 2012

At one o'clock in the morning, Jan sat up and asked Beryl, "Do you think we put enough stones around Prego's body?"

The question awakened and surprised Beryl. "You're dreaming!" she said. "Go back to sleep. We'll talk about it in the morning."

At breakfast, Jan checked first with Dolph's helicopter service company. The MD 500 was back inside the hangar. Not a single scratch was on it. He sighed with relief and called the hospital. Dolph was awake and able to speak. "They got the slug out. It missed my femoral artery by a millimeter. I can probably go home tomorrow. I had to get tetanus shots and a bunch of other 'preventative' things. It hurts."

"I checked with your company. Your MD 500 is back inside the hangar, safe and sound."

"Did you fly it back?" Dolph asked.

"Hell no. A lieutenant whose name I can't remember flew it back. Incidentally, Beryl tells me that your little sister is due to arrive from Brazil today. We'll go and pick her up at the airport, if that's ok with you."

"She's coming in from Sao Paulo at noon. I forget the flight number."

"No problem. Do you want us to drop by the hospital with her to see you?"

Beryl interrupted, "Ask him what school she should be taken to!"

Dolph heard the question and answered it, saying that he'd really like to see Juliana after they picked her up. "Thanks for remembering to do this. I appreciate it."

"It's our pleasure," Jan said. "Incidentally, your motorcycle and mine are both still down there. They're inside the manager's office. We'll talk about it later."

At the conclusion of the call, he looked at Beryl in a child-like way. "What is left to do?" he asked.

She pretended to consult a list. "Next you have to decide immediately whether or not you intend to turn those DVDs into evidence."

Jan groaned. "I can't think constructively about those damned things. What would you do? I'm sorry. That was my father in those videos. I may not be able to think straight for another hundred years. I'm in shock... just blitzed."

"This isn't something I can decide for you. What are the consequences of turning them in? Think about it. By the way, now that you're speaking again, I ought to tell you that Piet, Prego, the three women, and Juliana are not the only people in those films. There is another man... a darkish man with long straight hair. Nice looking. He looked like a native. Much taller than Prego. Prego could stand up everywhere in the cave. This guy had to bend over when he got to the sides. If they called him by name, I couldn't hear because I turned the volume down. You really need to look and listen to that part of the recording. He's got to know something about what's been going on down there."

Jan got up and pulled her to her feet. "Lay on, MacDuff," he said. "Let me see the part of the video that he's in."

Beryl put on latex gloves and retrieved the shopping bag from behind the couch. She selected one of the three "Prego" disks and inserted it into the player. She fast-forwarded the disk until she reached the midway point. The long-haired man came on the screen.

"I know him!" Jan sat up. "His name is Kepu Arare. He's native!" Jan watched Kepu sit, drink, and laugh at the proceedings with one of the whores. He took no part in tormenting her, but neither did he act to restrain her tormentors. "The son of a bitch just sits there, finding it funny. He has a huckstering boat... goes up and down the river selling soaps and thread and sharpens knives. I know where he lives. Jesus. He's not even known to be a troublemaker!"

Beryl turned off the DVD. "That's the only one he's in. I don't suppose there was much he could have done to stop it. As we have learned, one does not argue with Prego." She put the disk in its plastic case and returned all the disks to their place behind the couch. "If you decide that you don't want to turn in the DVD's, you and I better go down there again... as soon as possible... and search the cave thoroughly before you turn in your report. You don't want your forensics people to find another recording."

.

In the land of giants, eighteen year old Juliana Gerber could have passed as a toddler. She had a name and school printed on a tag which was pinned to her starched cotton coat-dress, and her reticule purse was pinned to her sleeve. Her long brown hair was braided into one long braid that trailed down her back all the way to her waist and ended with a bow tied around it. She wore long white stockings and flat Mary Jane shoes.

An airline employee escorted her to the custom's desk where Jan and Beryl waited. She smiled and clasped her hands together and said nothing.

Jan said, "We'll be taking you to see your brother."

"Adolph," she said.

"Yes, Adolph."

Jan and Beryl led her out to the Land Rover. Beryl buckled her into the passenger seat.

.

Dolph Gerber held his arms out to hug Juliana as she entered his room. His expression registered joy and gratitude. "How was your airplane ride?" he asked her.

"Fine," she said. "The same nurse that met me at the plane took me back to the plane. That was nice. I had breakfast before I left so I didn't get hungry on the plane."

"Are you hungry now?" he asked.

"I'd like some ice cream," she answered; and Beryl, who was standing in the doorway, signaled that she'd get a dish of ice cream for her at the cafeteria.

Jan pulled a chair along side Dolph's bed so that Juliana could sit down. "Beryl's getting some ice cream for you right now," Jan said.

Dolph Gerber whispered, "Thank you."

Jan patted his shoulder. "Do you want to us to notify your sister Andrea in Aruba?"

Gerber vehemently shook his head. "No."

Jan nodded. "We'll pick you up tomorrow to take you home."

Beryl returned with a small dish of ice cream and a spoon. She was surprised to see that Juliana did not seem to be able to feed herself. She wondered if the girl's muscles or shoulder joints had been damaged by prolonged use of restraints or by hanging by her wrists.

.

As soon as Juliana was safely back in her school, Jan called the military transport office at the airport and requested an early morning flight down to Kwamalasamutu.

When they returned to Jan's apartment they found the door to the patio open and several chairs askew. "Somebody was in here," Jan said, "and he probably retreated over the patio wall when he heard us open the front door."

Beryl was already checking behind the sofa. She pulled on a pair of latex gloves, picked up the bag, and counted through the disks to see that they were all there.

"Whoever it was is no doubt following us," Jan whispered in Beryl's ear. "Any ideas for keeping these disks safe?"

She looked up at him and nodded. She closed the draperies on all the windows and then led him into the bathroom and shut the door. She removed all of the disks from their plastic cases and whispered, "Your old fashioned bathroom is the perfect place to hide these. Get me some *Crazy Glue*."

Jan went to his desk and got a small tube of instant glue. Beryl inserted the disks under the chenille toilet lid cover and then, with a few dabs of glue, sealed the end so that the disks would not slide out. When the glue was dry, she put the toilet lid up and said, "There!" She returned the bag of empty cases to its place behind the sofa.

"Let's get ready for tomorrow's safari," Jan said, picking up her "Puss'n'Boots" footwear. He put his hand down inside one of the boots. "It's damp... wet, actually." He got a hair dryer and, turning the boot upside down, he let the heat rise into the boot.

Beryl smiled. "A domestic god! I really should kidnap you and make you my sex and housework slave."

"I will go willingly. No force is necessary." Suddenly he turned off the dryer. "Was he selling copies of these sexual child abuse tapes? Is that where he got his money? Maybe there are 'snuff' films down there. You looked at the complete DVD collection. Did you see what happened to those three women once they were done tormenting them?"

"Don't go inventing crimes. We don't know what happened to those women. If they were let go, it isn't likely that they'd complain to anyone knowing, as they do, that their ordeal was filmed. We just have to be sure that there are no other videos we missed. You've got to report the incident. Dolph was shot. He was rescued by a government helicopter. A bullet from your gun killed Prego. These are not details that you can overlook." She stood up and let him put his arms around her as his chest heaved as if it were trying to buttress his heart.

Finally he composed himself. "What's next on the list?" he asked. "I need direction. I've looked at people who seemed so confused when they were confronted by some terrible news about their family, and I used to feel so detached and superior. As if I'd have handled the news differently. I would never be so helpless. Christ! Look at me. Is this what you Zen people call 'karma'?"

"No." She tried not to sound patronizing. "This isn't payback. You're just another innocent victim. Call it tuition, but not karma. As soon as Dolph's home and not on any pain medication, we should discuss this whole business with him."

"I can't talk to him about this."

"Why not? It had nothing to do with you."

"The man was my father. I feel like vomiting every time I think about it. I have his genes. I'm not just shocked by seeing the handiwork of a child-molesting sadist. *This man was my father.*"

"And Greta Gerber was Dolph's mother! What do you think that suicide-murder was all about? Guilt! How could she not have known what was going on? Piet must have hated Juliana because her very existence made a fool of him. Greta probably hated her because the kid's father dumped Greta as soon as the pregnancy was known. An innocent kid became a scapegoat for all their sins. It sure does look like guilt and revenge."

"I've hesitated to ask you this... but did Dolph see that cache of DVDs?"

"No. He was shot before I saw them, and then, before we went up to the cave, he was taken away in the helicopter."

"Then we don't have to tell him... or anybody that we even found the DVDs."

"It's your call," Beryl said. "On one hand, knowing the full extent of her torment may be helpful to the psychiatrist who's treating her. But on the other hand, if he sees the videos and collapses under the burden of those images, he won't be much help to her. But, he may already know."

Jan groaned. "Jesus. Why did it have to be me who got involved in all this..." The question did not require an answer.

"How could you have known?" Beryl asked. "Your step-mother wanted you to be or to hire a private investigator. If you had told her that you didn't want anything to do with it, she'd have hired her own P.I. Would you have preferred that someone else find the disks?"

"She probably did hire another P.I. Who the hell broke into my apartment? Who knew we were gone at the time or where we had gone the day before? I've had a feeling we were being watched. I'm so sorry I got you mixed up in this. I agreed to help her for no other reason but that I wanted you to come down here. It seemed like a good idea at the time."

"Then that's what you should be focussing on. I'm glad you did. I'm glad I'm the one who's with you during a crisis like this."

"So am I," he said simply. "Now at least I don't have to worry about telling you what kind of blood runs in my veins."

"I am always mindful of Jonathan Swift's 'Modest Proposal,'" she said. "Your genes and chromosomes are of no interest to me since I am 'past child-bearing age.'"

He laughed. "On that goddamned list you're making of things I need to do, put 'Get a vasectomy' at the top."

"For the other, younger women in your life?"

Jan shook his head and tried to suppress a desire to laugh. "In the midst of chaos you can bring some cockeyed kind of order."

"There's another question you have to deal with. You called me down to investigate your father's conviction. I did and I came up with an alternate theory of the crime. That's all it is... a theory. But it probably is enough to get the courts to act... if only so that they can get Helena Osterhaus to go back to the Netherlands as quickly as possible. They might even resort to canonizing him if that would get her to board a KLM flight 'across the pond.' But before you do anything, you must talk to Dolph."

"Why?"

"Because you don't know what can of worms you'll be opening if you don't talk to him first. You don't know what he knows about the suicide. You don't know what he knows about the abuse. Why can't you talk to this man and find out what he knows and thinks?"

"But then there won't be two separate things... the suicide-murder and the child abuse DVDs. They'll be just what they are now, two parts of the whole. I'm an officer of the law, for Christ's sake. Under the theory that will absolve my father of murder, we'd be condemning Dolph's mother for a vicious, criminal act of spite. And if anybody starts to wonder what happened to the gun, we might even find Dolph complicit in the crime. No. I think I'll just forget about the DVDs. I won't discuss them with Dolph. Maybe I'll burn the goddamned things. Maybe I should just let the local constabulary find Prego's body or let the crocodiles have it. Dolph was shot by a wanted man... a fugitive. He doesn't know any more than that. Why tell him more?"

"You aren't thinking clearly. Are you not listening? There is a record of your involvement in the incident. You took a government helicopter to the site of a killing. A bullet from your gun killed Prego. You have in your possession jewelry that may solve the disappearances of innocent women. The police have the slug that was removed from Dolph's leg.

That slug once had a casing that may be lying on the ground down there with marks on it that match casings left at other crime scenes. An officer flew Dolph's helicopter back from the area. His motorcycle and yours are still there in the hangar manager's office. You just can't ignore what other people are talking about. Then there's the matter of Kepu."

"Kepu," Jan repeated. "That's what I'll do then. I'll go down tomorrow morning and find him. I will not be gentle. I will find out what the hell went on at that mine site. I will also go to the site and scour it and then make a report about it. If news of the disks gets out, I'll say that my apartment was burgled right after I brought the DVDs home and I didn't even see them."

"No, Jan. You've got to talk to Dolph. You two may decide to keep the DVDs secret. That's fine. Make sure there are no more videos hidden there and then let your forensics people document the crime scene. The crimes involving possibly missing women need to be attended to."

SATURDAY, MARCH 24, 2012

No rain had fallen through the night and the morning sky was bright. Large dark clouds had passed over the city but their threat had not been realized. All that was left in the sky were two white clouds that were outlined with gold in the rising sun. They moved farther apart, revealing more of the intense blue of the tropical sky.

After a breakfast that seemed almost sacramental in its silence, Beryl drove Jan to the military wing of the airport, and then she drove on to the hospital.

Dolph was sitting up, waiting.

"You're up pretty fast," she said.

"They even made me walk to the john," he said. "They don't want me to get blood clots or infections. If you think I don't feel like I've got an axe buried in my leg, you're wrong. An axe. A big one."

"I'm sorry I got you into this," she said. "I never expected to encounter what we encountered."

"I figured you were a cop... maybe an insurance cop... or bounty hunter," he whispered. "Thanks for getting Juliana at the airport. Oh, that other thing. Saving my life with the helicopter basket."

"You can thank Jan for that. He went back down to the site. In the meantime, we need to talk... you and I... alone and private... about your mother's suicide."

"I suppose there is no way to avoid it. I'll call the nurse and sign the release forms. We can talk back at my house."

Over tea served at the kitchen table, they began the discussion.

"Ever since Piet Osterhaus was convicted," Beryl said, "Jan's grandparents and Piet's wife Helena have been pressuring Jan to find evidence that would prove his innocence. But recently Helena has become even more persistent. Her daughters are now getting close to marriageable age and it isn't exactly a nuptial inducement to have a murderer hanging on the family tree. Jan had always ignored her requests. But as you know, a year ago I was down here on a case - that was before Piet died - and met Jan and one thing led to another between us. Then, as Piet's widow, Helena started to nag Jan incessantly. She demanded that if he wouldn't act, the least he could do was to hire a P.I. He was lonely and thought it would be a great way for us to get together. And here we are. He's on the verge of a nervous breakdown. Nobody expected to learn what we learned. And there's another wrinkle I should warn you about. Someone, probably Helena, has hired another P.I. to observe Jan and me. His apartment was broken into."

"What were they trying to find?"

"A bunch of sadistic child-abuse DVDs plus some other home-made porn. We brought the disks back."

"Did they get them?"

"No. They're secure now."

"Did you watch the DVDs?"

"Yes. Awful stuff. You don't want to see them... ever."

"I already saw one of them. What has happened since the time I got shot until now?"

"If I tell you will you give me the truth about the suicide?"

"Tell me what you already know."

"I wondered why your mom didn't have a clothes' dryer. Jan explained that folks down here often hang rugs outside and spray the back with bleach. But if that were the case, why would she have planted roses where those rugs would be hanging. The rest was easy. She was baking. Rats are everywhere in the tropics. I figured about the loaf of bread and the retractable cord... probably a dog leash tied to the pole. And the tipping rig for the potting soil and plants. I could come up with an alternate theory about the means of death. But I was stuck on motive. After seeing the DVDs I have motive. And the disappearance of the gun and even the tidy way the grave appeared when it was officially discovered lead me to assume that you're the one who removed the evidence."

Dolph nodded. "You've got it. That's pretty much exactly how it went. Andrea knew nothing about this. I heard her car pull up and didn't have time to get rid of the tipping board. As you know, she's remained loyal to Piet. Where did you find the DVDs?"

"Prego lived up on that ledge. Do you remember the ladder? Well, that ledge was a kind of cave. In it he had a generator that operated a DVD recorder, player, and monitor. Do you remember those plastic gasoline jugs? They were for the generator."

"What happened to that guy? The last thing I remember was that he asked me for keys. I've been afraid to ask anyone here for fear of starting something that I didn't want to finish. I've watched the news this morning... early. I saw nothing about it on TV."

"Jan killed him, not two minutes after Prego shot you. You were in terrible pain and bled a lot. Anyway, Prego was trying to force me to climb up to the cave. He was a few rungs beneath me on the ladder when Jan shot him. Luckily Jan had come down here following me independently and his official helicopter was still at the airfield. So they came and lowered a basket and we loaded you into it - and up, up and away you went. Then we searched the ledge and found the DVDs and a frightening amount of women's jewelry and garments."

"You think they brought women there and killed them?"

"That's possible. It's also possible that they robbed a few houses and gave items to girls in exchange for sex. Or a combination of both. They'll match up any items with missing person's reports. Jan will probably turn them in later today. Right now he's on his way back to the site to be sure we didn't miss any of the DVDs. He doesn't want forensics to get them. Tell me about the suicide."

"Is he certain that he won't be making the DVDs public?"

"Absolutely. But I want you to know that there may be other DVDs around. Also, there was another man involved in the videos. Not with Juliana's videos, but there are three other DVDs that show them torturing three women who looked like professionals. Prego is in the films with the three women who had come to the site under the impression, apparently, that they were going to service Piet. Instead, they got Prego. There was also a young native guy in one of the disks made in the cave. Jan recognized the man. And if this stupid case isn't closed quickly, Helena Osterhaus will keep digging. Jan and I are being followed. So don't say anything to the authorities. Give me a chance to give Jan the ability to find a solution to the mess that won't harm your sister even more."

"Where are the videos now?"

"I have them and they are safe."

"Did he see them?"

"He saw less than two minutes then went to vomit. He's a complete wreck."

"All right. What did you want to know?"

"When did you find out about what he was doing to Juliana?"

"I found out a month or so before she killed herself. September 2008.

"Piet had loaded his Piper to fly it down to the campsite. The weather was beautiful. It hadn't rained for days. He had six helicopters and a couple of Pipers in the fleet... all leased out. One of the Pipers that was leased to an important client developed engine trouble. Piet had to give him the plane he intended to use. I was at the field and helped him unload his gear. We put Piet's stuff inside the hangar since he intended to fly out the next day. I saw how protective he was of one satchel. I wondered what was in it. The client called him to come out so he could thank him personally for sacrificing his trip to accommodate him.

"When he went out to shake hands, I opened the satchel and saw the home made videos. There were two of them. I always wondered why he was so damned secretive about so much of his life. So I took a disk out of the box and closed the satchel. He was walking back towards the hangar. I could hear his footsteps. I had a western denim shirt on... with a breast pocket big enough to hold the DVD. It fit and there was no bulge. I said, 'Do you want me to help you load the stuff into your car?' He said, 'No.' I said, 'Should I tell Mom you'll be home for dinner?' 'Ok,' he said, 'tell her to make spaghetti.' He put his gear in a locker and got in his car and drove off.

"I went into the office and put the video in the player and watched it. I couldn't go home. I called and said a friend was picking me up to go to Aruba. I knew where the master key was to the lockers so I opened his and put the disk back into its case. I remembered to tell my mother to make spaghetti. I had to see a doctor. I couldn't stop shaking. I sat at the beach all night.

"The next day I went home. Piet's motorcycle was gone. I knew she was alone in the house. I told my mother I had seen the video. I could tell by the look on her face she knew all about it. She began to cry and asked me to forgive her. I slapped her face. Back and forth, five or ten times. I slapped her until I started to cry. I said, "If you say you permitted him to touch her because you needed the money to support Andrea and me, I will kill you. I meant it.

"I asked her, 'How could you do that to Juliana?' She told me that the 'dummkopf' - that means stupid head, like a mentally retarded child - was the source of all the grief in her life, that if she hadn't gotten pregnant with her, her life would have been so wonderful. 'I had Satan inside me,' she said. 'Because of her, your father threw me out onto the street. Because of her Piet beat me and filmed it and forced me to do terrible things. Because of her I've had to live like a prisoner. He threatened to tell my family back in Germany and Juliana's father's family... everybody I knew. Because of her he put a lien on my house. I can't sell it.' I asked how he was able to put a lien on the house and she told me that she was able to pay for Andrea's and my college tuition with a loan from him that he made her sign. She said she had to have receipts for every penny of household expense - and also for the businesses that were in her name. He'd deduct one-third for his own part of the household expense, and then when she amassed enough receipts, he would take her to the bank and she would sign a promissory note and he would put money into her account which she would spend until she needed another loan. She had to use the house as collateral. To my mother, every single problem she faced could be blamed on somebody else. She was never responsible for her own actions. She kept saying, 'I should have had an abortion. If I knew then what I know now, I'd have killed her the day she was born.'

"That night she took an overdose of pills. I forced ipecac down her throat. I made her drink strong coffee and walk. I wouldn't take her to the hospital. She kept saying, 'I want to die. I want to die.' I said that she should find a way to take him to hell with her. I hated her and him enough to kill them both."

"And who can blame you. Jesus. An innocent child."

"After my father threw her out, she could have ended the pregnancy; but she caught Piet's eye and she saw a way to make the pregnancy work to her advantage. He was the perfect patsy. He was handsome and well liked, a pilot and a gold prospector. By marrying him she thought she could spite them all. She convinced him that the baby was his. He went around bragging about it. My father filed for divorce, but he dragged it out until after Juliana was born so that Piet wouldn't be duped the way he was. But by then the house was already built and put in her name as Piet's loving gift to her. Piet really looked forward to family life. Juliana destroyed that possibility. Greta had made a fool of him. He made them both pay."

"Did he know who Juliana's biological father was?"

"Yes, but I never learned his name. The night I confronted my mother, I was told that Piet knew the guy but did not like him. Though the guy knew Juliana was his kid, he refused to pay any support for her. My father did. DNA tests were possible; but Piet had no legal standing since my dad supported Juliana and acknowledged her as his daughter.

"Piet became the object of jokes at his clubs and the bars he hung out in. Juliana's biological father would mock Piet for being such a sucker and actually laughed in his face.

"Piet's initial response was to go to Amsterdam and get married. But then he had to come back here to earn money panning for gold and hiring out as a bush pilot. And the guy, whoever he was, kept laughing at him.

"So Piet got even with the guy in other ways. Every time he abused Juliana, he was paying him back. Then, on Sundays he would take Juliana and my mother out in public and Juliana always seemed mentally defective. And Piet would be sure the guy saw her and then he'd smirk. *Quid pro quo.*

"All those years I thought that my sister was mentally retarded. They had driven her crazy. He had even taken her to some special clinic in Peru to have electric shock therapy. After he was in jail for a year, I was looking through his papers and found the hospital receipts. I went to see him to find out how many shock treatments she had had. I supposed they wanted to obliterate her memories of the abuse. He asked me when did I first learn of Juliana's abuse. I told him. He asked if I had helped his mother to frame him. I said, 'Yes.' He said, 'Well, I don't blame you. In one stroke you got her, me, and the bitch in Amsterdam.' He asked what the doctors had said about Juliana's recovery. I said it depended on how many ECT treatments she had had. He said she had only one. I told him that if that were the case, the doctors said that it's possible that she will recover. But she is living in a special home... an expensive one. He said, 'You can afford it now.'"

"What is the surgical procedure Juliana had in Brazil?"

"She puts straight pins and needles in her thighs. This time they removed twenty-seven needles. The time before it was thirty-six. Before that it was forty-nine. I guess you could see the decline as an improvement."

"Where does she get the needles?"

"She steals them from a seamstress in her school. I don't have the heart to tell them what she does with them."

"Poor kid. I didn't mean to interrupt your story. What happened next?"

"I thought up the roses and the leash and the loaf of bread. When I bought the leash, I also bought a few food rats. To this day I don't know where I got the idea. It just came to me. I set it up for her and then I went away for a few days over the holiday for my alibi. I didn't know whether she had gone ahead with it or not. It was like a defendant must feel waiting for a verdict. I couldn't breathe. If she didn't do it, I'd think of something else. If she did, my concern was that Andrea would get home before me and that the grave wouldn't look like a grave. But it looked pretty good. I didn't have to do much to it... just straighten the bushes. The rats ate everything and leveled the potting soil as they scurried around on it. I took the board and tipping rock away. I took the gun down from the pole. I went back in the house to wait for Andrea. Just in time. She came in the front door before my hands were dry from washing the dirt off."

"What did you do with the gun?"

"While flying over the ocean, I tossed it out the window."

"I can't tell you what to do," Beryl said, "but if you want my opinion, it is not to tell anyone that you had any part in the plan. It's a complicated crime... but a crime nevertheless. Disposing of the gun is a felony... and probably assisting in her suicide - by buying the leash - not to mention the rats - is also gonna get you jail time. If you're convicted, who will look after Juliana?

"This 'alternate theory of the crime' may come to light. Helena's other private investigators no doubt know that you and I went down to that mining site. All that DVD equipment may still be there. Prego's dead. But he isn't the only man in the videos... there's a young native. Jan is going down today to interrogate him in a subtle way. Meanwhile, think of another reason why your mother might have wanted to take her own life and set Piet up for murder, and also try to find another way that the gun could have been removed from the back yard."

"She did have German friends. They could have helped her. But what about Jan? Did you tell Jan about your theory of the crime?"

"Yes. He wasn't entirely convinced. He wondered why your mother would do that... it seemed like such a spiteful thing to do... until he saw the videos. Then it made more sense than the murder version."

"What does Jan intend to do?"

"Let you decide. He keeps referring to his father's genes. He thinks he should get a vasectomy."

"Tell him that I know exactly how he feels. For the videos that were made in our house, it was my mother who held the camera."

"Good grief! Well, there are many innocent victims out there because of the whole sordid mess. He feels sorry for his two half-sisters."

"What do you think we should do?"

"I don't think that revealing the abuse is going to help anyone. If his daughters are not marriageable because their father is a murderer, their prospects will not be improved by absolving him of that crime and convicting him of being a sadistic child abuser. Juliana may recover. What will that information do to her? I think you and Jan need to settle things between you."

"Helena won't drop the matter. She'll dig and dig until the story comes out. You figured it out; so will one of her hired detectives. We need to find a plausible reason for my mother's actions. Maybe Piet told her he was going back to Amsterdam to be with Helena. Maybe they had a fight and he told her he was dumping her and taking away all the money he had intended to leave her and us. She needed the money for Juliana's care. Saying that he was going back to Helena would work unless Helena knows he probably hated her."

"That woman is so vain, she'd regard it as Gospel that he loved her and intended to come back and beg her to forgive him, et cetera, et cetera."

"My sister Andrea believed in Piet's goodness. She must have suspected abuse, but I think she would prefer to think that it was Mom who was abusing her. Andrea always sided with my step-father. He rewarded her handsomely for her love and loyalty."

"Andrea and Helena will gloat about poor Piet… they always knew he was innocent! And you'll just have to sit there and listen to it. You and Jan. Ah… if the courts do give credence to the alternate theory of the crime, you'll have to witness 'The apotheosis of Piet Osterhaus.' Maybe you should have an angel sculpted to put over his gravesite."

"You mean… take the one away I had sculpted for my blessed mother's gravesite… and move it to his?"

"You didn't!"

"Yes… I ordered an angel for her gravesite. It cost eighteen thousand dollars. Italian marble." He laughed and in the tension of the moment the laugh became a giggling hysterical laugh. His phone rang. Still laughing, he spoke to Jan. After a minute, he handed the phone to Beryl.

"What was all that laughing about?" Jan asked.

"About the alternate theory - the one that will absolve Piet and tend to make a saint of him. Dolph said he ought to move the statue of an angel he had made for his mother's grave to Piet's grave."

Jan did not quite understand the humor.

Dolph once again burst out laughing. "Carrara marble," he wheezed and gulped. "The kind Michelangelo used."

.

Beryl returned to the apartment to find the plastic cases strewn all over the living room floor. Fearing that she might be being watched, she did not run to the bathroom to see if the disks were there. Instead, she put on rubber gloves and returned the cases to the shopping bag.

Jan called her on her iPhone. "What was that all that laughing about?" he asked.

"Actually," Beryl said, "it was Dolph's joke. I don't want to talk on the phone. Somebody broke in and went through the shopping bag of empty DVDs. When will you be back?"

"Tonight. I'm on the sat phone and the line's secure. Tomorrow we'll have to rekey the doors and maybe get security cameras. I've got a lot to tell you. Does Dolph know why I'm down here?"

"Generally, yes."

"He must have been as shocked as I was."

"He apparently was."

"So he's ok if we go ahead and reveal the alternate theory?"

"Yes. The reason she killed herself and tried to blame Piet was that he told her he was going to dump her and go back to Helena. Ah, she was so heartbroken and bitter. Maybe one of her friends from Germany helped her and retrieved the gun."

"Incidentally, Prego's gravestones were scattered. His remains are gone. Remind me never to eat caiman. Ok. I'll be home later. Wait up for me. Oh, there's one other thing. Dolph will have to back up the alternate theory with some kind of statement that his mother was indeed disturbed about something but that he had assumed it was just another domestic dispute - that old 'will' story. He can give a few details that now, in the light of this new version of events, take on relevance. For example, Piet gave him certain personal items... hunting knives, a motorcycle, a leather jacket, things a man would want to pass on to a son if he intended to leave permanently."

"I'm sure he'll go along with that."

"Ask him but don't go public with the story. I need to think about this. Since you got down here I've broken a few hundred laws. I'm not supposed to break the law. We need to go into my office and make official statements. We can say we delayed because of food poisoning. We have to turn in the rifle, jewelry, and garments that were in the cave. I removed all the DVD recording equipment. Not the player, just the DVD burner. I won't turn in the DVD stuff. Everything else, yes."

"What did you find out about Kepu?"

"Nothing yet. We'll see."

.

Kepu Arare huckstered needles, thread, toiletries, soaps, tools, lamp oil and mosquito netting on his large canoe; and he also had a grinding wheel and honing stones that earned him a good income from sharpening machetes.

Jan had not acted as though it were anything important that he wanted to talk to Kepu about. When he approached the village captain and asked if he knew where Kepu was, he casually explained, "Nobody knows the river communities the way he does. I want him to give me his input about the best place for the government to put a small storage and exchange center on the river. Native input is always helpful." He did not want to scare Kepu into fabricating excuses or denials about possible charges.

The captain believed him and inquired about Kepu's itinerary. He looked at his watch and guessed that Kepu was probably about 10 kilometers upriver. He did not know how many little stops the huckster would be making.

Jan thanked him and said he'd wait for him by the river, outside the Shattuck Falls shack - in case the captain saw him before Jan did.

Jan had already gone to the mine site. He was relieved and not at all surprised to find that Prego's body was gone. He climbed up to the ledge and explored the cave, moving loose rocks and piles of debris as he searched for more videos. He found a set of screwdrivers and sat down close to the ladder where the light was best and methodically took a DVD duplicating machine apart. The parts that were metal he put aside, the rest he tossed down into a pile. When it was completely taken apart, he tossed down the box of blank DVD disks since it was too large for him to carry out. Then he climbed down, poured gasoline over the plastic parts and DVD blanks and ignited the pile. A breeze blew the black smoke away from him and he was able to wait patiently until the pile was reduced to a twisted mass of unrecognizable blobs. He shoveled the remains into a wheelbarrow and pushed it to the downstream rapids. There again, using the shovel, he threw the mangled bits of plastic into the swift current.

The metal parts of the duplicating equipment presented another problem. He climbed the ladder and, sitting in the sunlight, proceeded to obliterate the serial numbers and other identifying marks on the metal pieces, flattening or bending them until they were unrecognizable. Several times he cut his hands in his zeal to destroy the evidence of what he regarded as his personal dereliction of duty. He put the pieces into an evidence bag, intending to dispose of them when he returned to the city. He found a business card that had come from Dolph's wallet and put it in his pocket, and he placed the rifle and as many shell casings as he could find into an evidence bag. He also collected whatever clothing, shoes, and purses that were in the cave and placed them in one bag. Aside from the manufacturers' labels, the items had no identifying marks. Perhaps, he thought, DNA could be retrieved from them and could put to rest a family's worries. He tried to limit the contact his hands had with anything that he had removed from the cave, but soon the impossibility wore down his resolve. He sincerely considered the possibility that contracting a disease would be some kind of divine and completely justified punishment. How could he have been so oblivious to his own father's life?

It was approaching 2 p.m. as he sat on one of the logs that passed for outdoor furniture of the shack that passed for a general store in Shattuck Falls' little outpost. Word would probably get to Kepu that he was waiting for him. And then, inevitably, Kepu would try to anticipate the questions he would be asked and would, accordingly, prepare the most self-serving answers.

This, Jan knew, was the down side of wearing a uniform. Nobody ever gave a straightforward answer. People did not respond to the man, they responded to the uniform, needing always to defend themselves against an attack or to ingratiate themselves on those rare occasions when credit was to be gained. Jan knew that if Kepu were aware that he was waiting to ask him questions, he would approach the NBI officer as a beginner studies a chess board. "If he does this, then I will do that; but if he does the other, then I will do this." He would try to manipulate the uniform.

The discovery of his father's barbarity made Jan feel unworthy to interrogate a native who was only minimally involved. He cursed himself for his arrogance and laughed at the irony. "Here I am... going to demand that he give me the truth as though the truth were important. Why should he give me anything that I wasn't even professional enough to work for... to inquire about... to show the slightest doubt or curiosity about when the so-called facts were presented to me. I accepted the most far-fetched lies, but from him I will demand brutal truth?"

Hearing a canoe's motor coming towards him as it proceeded upstream in Kepu's direction, he got up and retreated to the rear of the shack. He did not want anyone to warn Kepu that he was waiting outside.

Sitting on a log he noticed that a clump of mud had adhered to the instep of his shoe. It looked like mud from the mine site, and wanting to wipe it off, he reached into a cluster of bromelia leaves to pick one to use as a wipe. As he broke the jagged stem, he noticed a tiny flash of sapphire blue pass under his lacerated palm and felt a brushing sensation. He jerked his hand back and examined it. He didn't know whether a piece of the stem had touched him or whether it was the frog. Few creatures in the world were as poisonous as the bright colored dart frogs. A single yellow cousin of the blue could kill a dozen men. A child, so touched, would die. Adults who survived would suffer irreversible organ damage. Natives often rubbed their darts on the skin of the frog and nothing the dart struck ever survived. In a confused panic, he got up and went to the river and stooped down to wash his hand. It was a natural, though pointless, attempt to rid himself of the poison. There was no antidote. Either his palm had been touched or it had not. It was that simple.

If the frog had touched him, he did not want to fall forward into the water. While he could still move, he retreated to the log and sat down, waiting to see if he would feel the effects of the neurotoxin... the paralysis. It astonished him to think that such an innocuous act as picking a leaf could end his life. Luck? Was everything luck? A silly thought came to his mind. Luck. Lucky. "I'm waiting for God-O. Oh, Me-O, My-O," he sang the words like a ditty. "I'm waiting for God-O." Beckett aside, he could only wait. Nothing seemed to be happening.

As he sat there feeling suspended between being and non-being, a voice inside his head asked, "Is this all there is? Is this all there is to life?" He became aware of the cosmic indifference to his existence. His life was inconsequential. What was it for, this life without meaning? Was it a divine joke? How could so much depend on the luck of the moment - the clump of mud, the desire to wipe it off, the decision to use a leaf to wipe it, the presence of a dart frog among those leaves, and, above all, the height of that frog's jump. Did it jump high enough to brush his hand? How much of life depended on stupid luck like this?

Was this all there was to life? To end up sitting on a log, waiting to learn whether a pretty blue frog was going to kill him with a touch, like the hand of God. "Is this all there is to life?" he asked himself repeatedly. He heard his name being called.

Kepu was standing in his boat coming towards him. "Did you wanna talk to me?" he shouted.

Jan got up. "Yes," he called.

As the prow of the motor-canoe nosed into the dock, Jan, the man, seemed to vanish. What was left was the uniform's training and

75

experience. He walked to the water's edge, waiting to catch the line and tie it down.

Kepu Arare tossed the line. "Hey, Captain. What can I do you for?" he jauntily asked.

"I need to talk to you about something important."

Kepu, handsome, young, and with a brilliant smile, hopped onto the dock. "What's up?" he asked.

Jan motioned for him to sit on the log beside him. "What can you tell me about a guy named Prego?"

"Nuthin' much. He lives on one of your old man's mining sites. He lives up on a ledge... in a kind of cave."

"Oh... yeah... I saw that hideaway. He has a ladder that goes up to it."

"That's right. A ladder. But the gold is played out. I think he goes there because nobody wants him around. He's not too appetizing to look at." He laughed.

"What have you heard about taking women up there in that cave and doing nasty things to them? And don't say, 'nuthin',' because I've seen you in one of their films. Right now I'm trying to help you because I've always liked you and your folks. Some people are trying to put the blame on you for a lot of bad stuff. So don't lie to me. I won't lift a finger to help you if you lie."

The "caught criminal's" great dilemma confounded Kepu. Should he absolutely deny all knowledge of the crime or should he clean up the truth enough to eliminate or at least mitigate his part in it. He decided on the latter approach. "There was a Venezuelan whore who stole money from her pimp and tried to hire someone around here to kill him. She tangled with Prego. Prego doesn't like whores. He teaches 'em a lesson. I was there. I should have tried to stop him... but we were drinkin'."

"What happened to the woman?"

"I don't know. I had to get back. She looked beat-up but was still kickin' when I left."

"And what about the gold Piet used to take out of that placer mine? Where did it come from, Kepu? I know, but if I'm gonna trust you, I have to know that you're trustworthy."

"It was melted down stuff that different gangs stole from pawn shops and from robbin' people's houses. But Prego wasn't the fence, Piet was."

"What work did Prego do for Piet? And be careful how you answer. Give me a wrong answer and I'm gonna take you in."

"He made copies of porno disks. Hard Core stuff. Piet made a few dozen first edition disks that he called 'masters.' Sometimes Piet traded a master DVD and a few dollars for jewelry that the gangs stole, and they would copy and distribute the DVDs in Brazil, Peru, Bolivia, Venezuela... you name it. It was a big joke... his minin'. When he'd melt down the gold chains and rings he'd laugh about it. He got a lot of diamonds, too, out of those tradeoffs. Pearls. Opals. The guys who robbed the pawn shops and the private homes could never get more than 20% of their value if they tried to fence them locally. But they could make a fortune selling Piet's pornos because it wasn't phony ham actors pretending shit. It was real S&M... real stuff. Hey, Captain, I'm sorry to have to tell you about your old man... but you asked."

"What did my father do with the diamonds?"

"I think he sold them to a jeweler in Medellin. Full price. He had a French last name. I saw it once on a bag. 'Mont–' something. Piet always did well in those sales... he'd include a few free pornos.

"That's about all I know. Sometimes if one of the gangs was trying to find Piet's place and got lost, I'd guide them in. He'd tip me well."

"For your sake I'm telling you to keep this conversation to yourself. I told your village captain I wanted your opinion on a good place for the government to put a storage and service center. What do you think?"

"I think here at Shattuck Falls is the best place around. It's a little higher. The river's wider but shallower here."

"Ok, Kepu. Remember what I said. And stay away from the cave. There'll be government people all over it shortly." His tone changed. "How about giving me a lift downriver. Think you got room on that department store you ferry around?"

He called the airfield and told them he'd be there in an hour to make the return flight to Paramaribo. Meanwhile, they should load both motorcycles into the helicopter. When he disconnected the call he thought of Beryl's 'pretended s.o.s. calls.' He began to laugh. Then the relief of not being touched by the damned frog struck him and he really laughed. Kepu Arare grew afraid, thinking that the laugh was demoniacal. "What are you laughing at?" he asked warily.

Jan spoke to him man-to-man for the first time. "I've got a woman back in Paramaribo. She needed to come down into the bush and I was afraid for her and wanted to give her a satellite phone. She didn't want to take it. She said the things that scared her down here wouldn't be helped by a satellite phone. Then she pretends to call me–" - he imitated her voice - "*Hello Jan, an anaconda is wrapping itself around me. What should I do?*" He laughed. "*Hello Jan, a crocodile has me in its mouth and I can't read the GPS coordinates to tell you where I'm being consumed.*" And then he and Kepu began to laugh heartedly together. Jan was laughing so hard he could barely speak. "And I put my hand over her mouth to keep her from saying things that were making me laugh. So the first chance she gets, she says, '*Hello Jan, I'm being eaten by piranha. How soon can you get here?*'"

Kepu tried to control his laughter to add one to the list. "*Hello Jan, I've just found the cutest yellow frog. Can I bring it home?*" Again, they both laughed merrily.

As Jan settled down sitting there in Kepu's boat, he knew, somehow, someway, that suddenly he and Kepu were both better men than they had been before. The laugh was at God's joke, and the laugh had made them friends.

.

Before Jan went into his office to make a formal report of the incident involving Dolph's wounds and Prego's death, Beryl succeeded in getting him to agree to visit Dolph to discuss the disposition of the DVDs. First, however, he insisted on going to his apartment to bathe and dress.

As they drove home, Beryl gave him her impression of Dolph's position and responsibility in the whole affair.

"Well," she said, "one day in 2008, Dolph was suspicious about the way Piet guarded a particular satchel," and she continued on through the story of the revelation, Greta's attempted suicide, and Dolph's insistence that Greta find a way to do it and to take Piet with her. "The roses, the leash, the loaf of bread, and the tipped over board of potting soil were all his ideas. He gave her Piet's gun and went away to establish an alibi. He didn't know if she'd go through with it, but she did. He retrieved the gun and straightened the gravesite. End of story.

"Your guess about how Piet would react when he found out that the baby wasn't his was right on target. He didn't like being the butt of jokes and, initially, he tried to just get away from it. Hence, marriage in Amsterdam. But he had to come back to earn money. When the jokes continued, especially from Juliana's biological father - a guy Piet personally detested - he got even with him by taking it out on Juliana and Greta who, all along, had blamed the baby for all her misfortunes."

"Who was the baby's real father?"

"Dolph never learned his name. Greta told him that Piet threatened to show him porno pics of her that Piet had taken, but Dolph said she was a first class liar. Juliana was born while Greta was still married to Gerber, so she had his last name and Gerber supported the baby. It was a decent thing to do. I suppose that ultimately that is why Piet was good to Dolph and Andrea... and so bad to Juliana. What did you learn down at the cave?"

"As I approached the camp I couldn't detect decomp in the air. I knew the crocs had eaten the body. Remind me never to eat caiman."

"They must have been starving."

"No doubt. I burned a box of DVD blanks and the non-metal parts of the duplicating machine. I mangled the metal parts and put them in a bag which I tossed into the trash at the airport. I've got all the clothing and shoes from the site and I picked up the rifle and a bunch of casings. I'll turn them in with the jewelry."

"So what's left for forensics?"

"The monitor, the generator, and I took some of my old DVD's from home... old movies... to stick in the slot. He had to be using the equipment for something. I just didn't want someone to ask why he could play DVDs but didn't have any DVDs to play."

"Good thinking. What about Kepu?"

"Piet swapped DVDs of his child abuse and whore beatings to gangs of thieves from all around. They'd rob pawn shops and private homes and rather than get caught with the stolen property or get only a small percent of its value from fences, they swapped it for masters of the DVDs which they then copied and sold and made a whole lot more money than their thievery got them. Piet would melt the gold down and sell the jewels to a French jeweler he knew in Medellin. The jewels weren't 'fenced' in that sense of the word. He got full price for the stones but the buyer got a bonus of porn flicks. So he invested some of that money in legitimate businesses. I guess he had to account for his wealth."

.

At the Gerber house they sat in the kitchen and continued to discuss their "unified" response. "I've been thinking," Dolph said. "Until we decide what to do about my mother and Piet, why don't you file your report about the campsite? Do you have a reason for following us down?"

Beryl had a suggestion. "We can tell the truth. Jan asked me to investigate the murder/suicide death of Greta Gerber because Helena Osterhaus was driving him crazy demanding that he clear his father's name. I looked up Dolph pretending to be a journalist interested in Piet's success as a placer miner. Dolph agreed to take me down there so I could photograph the site... and the rest is history."

Jan interjected. "But I have legitimate concerns there, too. There was talk about building a government station on the river and since crime in that area is under my jurisdiction I thought I'd kill two birds with one stone and go down too. I was also afraid that my woman would get herself into trouble... being a tenderfoot and all.

"She had been instrumental in solving a case down here a year or so ago, so I had a GPS beacon put in your cycle... maybe jealousy had a little to do with it... but I'm serious about this woman. Marriage serious. I wanted to be sure I could be able to help her if she needed it. I knew about some of the lawlessness in that part of the 'three-corners' national borders. Turns out that she did need help. The NBI had never been able to pinpoint the place where so much mischief was occurring. Since it

involved my late father's placer mine, I was more than interested. I arrived
at the site just after Prego shot you."

"Then," Dolph said, "everything occurred exactly as it did occur."

Everyone agreed. To be absolutely certain, Jan said, "We saw a few
old DVD movies in the cave, but nothing else... just a DVD player and a
monitor. For the record," he whispered, "I destroyed all the duplicating
equipment. It never existed. I looked everywhere I could think of looking,
and I could find no more DVDs anywhere on the site. I brought all the
blanks out and burned them."

"Duplicating?" Dolph asked.

Jan looked at Beryl. "I guess you didn't know. That's how Piet made
his money." He reviewed the scheme.

"So what you're saying is that Piet duplicated the videos he made of
sexually molesting my sister?"

"Yes. Beryl saw them. I didn't."

Beryl could see how the news alarmed Dolph. "She will remain
anonymous in the DVDs. They ended when she was just starting puberty.
She's grown and gained weight and doesn't look anything like she looked
then. Those images might as well be of a stranger."

"My own mother held the camera."

Beryl raised her hands. "Enough! His own father was under that
Devil mask. They're both dead now, and you two have got to leave them
to God's judgment."

Jan got up. "Tomorrow we can talk more. I have to make a formal
report now. I'll be by in the morning to let you know how it went."

.

Jan, with Beryl silently following him, went directly to his office.
While she sat on a chair at the side of the room, Jan, wearing latex gloves,
showed the bagged rifle, garments, and jewelry to his superior and placed
them on the floor beside the wall. "There's nothing much left down there
for a forensics team to find. He had a bed and a monitor up on a ledge he
lived on. And a generator to run the movies he watched."

His supervisor seemed hostile. He buzzed in three members of a
forensics' team, one of whom was a young woman who had recently

been elevated to the rank of forensics 'specialist.' "Give them the GPS coordinates," he said to Jan. "And suppose you tell me why, when this happened on Thursday, you didn't get around to reporting it until Saturday night."

"On Thursday," Jan explained, "as the aviation logs will reveal, we had to airlift Dolph Gerber to a hospital. The man Prego - he's in the 'wanted' databases - shot Mr. Gerber. A Lieutenant flew Mr. Gerber's MD 500 helicopter back to Paramaribo. That's in the record, too. I had placed a GPS indicator in Mr. Gerber's motorcycle and was able to follow him and Miss Tilson. I arrived just after Gerber was shot and as Prego was attempting to rape Miss Tilson. I shot and killed him.

"In the excitement of evacuating Dolph Gerber I overlooked his personal possessions - keys and cards that Prego had taken out of Gerber's wallet. So I returned to get those keys and credit cards before any locals wandered onto the scene. I wanted to do this on Friday morning, but Dolph Gerber's little sister was flying in from Brazil where she had undergone a surgical procedure. I called airport authorities and agreed that Miss Tilson and I would wait for her arrival and take her to Gerber's hospital room and then to her school. Therefore I returned to the crime scene this morning."

"So you left Prego's body at the site?"

"Yes, but it's gone. We covered it with as many rocks as we could find, but the crocs made short work of the gravesite. When I arrived, there was no trace of the body and the rocks were scattered."

"What is all that stuff you've brought back?" The supervisor nodded to the young woman who started to reach for the jewelry bag with her bare hand.

"Ah! Ah!" Beryl suddenly spoke. Everyone turned and looked at her. "Don't touch that stuff, Miss," Beryl cautioned. "Don't touch any of it. And I don't think you should go down to the site, either. It is much too risky for you."

The girl did not know how to respond; but the supervisor was clearly annoyed. "All of our officers," he said stiffly, "are prepared to take whatever risks are inherent in an assignment."

"Of course they are," Beryl said. "But why let her risk anything? A hazmat team is one thing. But I can see by the casual way she wanted to handle the evidence, that you folks don't appreciate the kind of disease that's down there."

"I think we can approach the problem without any foreign advice," the supervisor said.

Beryl had noticed a large TV screen that could display photographs that were on his computer. "May I?" she asked, taking out her iPhone. She connected her iPhone to his computer and showed the first photo she had taken of Prego.

"What is it?" the supervisor asked.

"The man who Jan shot... Prego," Beryl said in a matter-of-fact tone.

"That's a man?" the young woman said. "My God!" she exclaimed, when she finally recognized the head and face of a man.

Beryl showed photographs of the chancre sores and lesions on his penis and testicles and the herpes and other blisters that covered his body. "Jan says the body's gone... eaten probably. The generator was a small one and if one of the locals finds it and the DVD player and disks, let him have it. There's nothing else there. The jewelry and purses may, however, belong to women who have been reported missing." She turned to the girl. "I was exposed to all this stuff. So was Jan. The site was seen from the air by your Air Force helicopter personnel. There's nothing to gain but a lot to lose if you go back there. In short, while I'm past child bearing age, you're not... and any one of the diseases that you might inadvertently get down there might affect your reproductive life." She returned to her chair. "But that's just a foreigner's advice."

"Well," the supervisor responded, "we'll interview Mr. Gerber and the man who airlifted him and saw the site up close and if the stories are all in agreement, we'll probably just pass on this." He continued to look at the photos of Prego. "Maybe we can send one of your Cruise missiles to the site instead of a forensics' team. Jesus! Look at that man!"

He called a hazmat officer and asked that the evidence be safely prepared for examination by the missing person's department.

No mention was made of alternate theories of the Gerber murder/suicide incident.

When they left NBI headquarters Beryl noticed a man in a straw hat leaning against the wall. She recalled that she had seen him earlier. "Is this the guy who's following us?" she asked Jan.

He looked around. "I know that guy," he said. "He's a P.I., a disreputable one. Helena's hero."

SUNDAY MARCH 25, 2012

Beryl and Jan got up late Sunday morning, determined to give themselves a few hours away from the case. They tried to talk about the weather and the latest Hollywood films but their conversation trailed into silence. "We've got an 800 pound gorilla prowling the patio," Beryl said.

Jan's phone rang and he gratefully picked it up. When he saw that it was Helena Osterhaus who was calling, he quietly put it down. "I'll let it go to voicemail," he said.

Helena's voice called from the street. "I know you're there. Come to the door!"

Beryl pretended to rub her eyes. *"Toto, I don't think we're in Kansas anymore."* She held Jan's arm. "Hold her off a minute. I want to check with Dolph."

Dolph spoke with greater conviction. "I've thought about the 'alternative theory.' I think it's a worthwhile effort. Too many innocent young people have already suffered. It's ok with me to present the theory."

She ended the call and looked at Jan. "Green light on the new theory. Go get 'em, tiger."

Jan shrugged impotently and went to his front door. Helena marched in, and with his two half-sisters trailing her, went directly to the patio and sat down. "I called," she said to Beryl, "to give Jan and you, if you were still here, time to make yourselves decent." The table had four chairs and, with Beryl, Helena, and the two girls sitting down, Jan folded his arms and leaned against the patio's stone wall.

Elise and Gretchen were more somber than they had previously been. Helena, too, seemed less imperious.

"Would you ladies care for some tea?" Beryl asked.

85

"No," Jan said. "They wouldn't. Mrs. Osterhaus no doubt has an appointment with the private investigator she hired... you know, the one who's been following us."

"Jan," Helena began in a soft voice, "I wasn't aware that you knew it was I who hired that awful man. I'm so sorry."

"Tell me, did you know he broke into this house yesterday?"

Helena hesitated, looking helplessly at her hands as she decided whether or not she should admit that she had something to do with a break-in. "I assure you," she said with her voice steeped in regret, "I had no idea that he would invade your home. Please forgive me. He said that he didn't take anything. If he did, please let me know and I'll reimburse you."

"If something turns up missing I'll be sure to send you a bill."

"I should apologize for hiring him. I thought that you were not seriously pursuing the restoration of your father's name. I hired him to supplement your investigation... in a manner of speaking."

"So what did your money buy you?"

"Nothing. I paid him off. He won't be following you anymore."

"So what you hired him to do was investigate Miss Tilson and me, to follow us, to see what we were doing."

"He came to me and told me that you were investigating one of your father's gold operations. I told him that I wasn't interested in any gold. I just wanted my husband's good name restored. He said that maybe the gold had something to do with Piet's being blamed for killing that woman. I'm appealing to you. Children can be so mean to one another. The story of Greta Gerber's murder is common knowledge in Amsterdam. My girls, who have done nothing, are being harassed. They are subjected to such cruel remarks. They come home and they are crying, begging me to free their Papa from this awful charge. They did not know him well, but they loved him. Perhaps if I had been a better wife, he'd have stayed in Amsterdam, and none of this would have happened. But I know in my heart that he is innocent. Can you do nothing for us?"

Jan looked at Beryl and then looked skyward. Resignedly he said, "I have news that should comfort you. Miss Tilson here has established a theory of the crime that does in fact absolve... Piet Osterhaus."

Helena gasped. "Oh! I can't believe it!" She looked at Beryl. "Please... please forgive my earlier rudeness. I beg you. Please. What have you learned? I've waited so long to hear the truth."

Jan answered, speaking very slowly. "Perhaps Greta Gerber was angry with... Dad... for wanting to return to you and the girls in Amsterdam."

"But what is the theory that Miss Tilson developed?" Helena asked, looking directly at Beryl.

Particularly because of Jan's preamble, Beryl did not feel that it was her place to explain the theory. She turned to Jan. "Why don't you give Dolph a quick call and ask if it's ok to visit the back yard now with Mrs. Osterhaus and her daughters."

Jan went inside his apartment to make the call. When he returned to the patio he had the keys to the Land Rover in his hand. "Come on," he said. Beryl picked up a folder of crime scene photos and the dog leash and followed them all out to the car; and, with Helena sitting in the passenger's seat and Beryl squeezed between the girls in the seat behind, they drove to the Gerber house.

In the back yard, with Dolph standing on crutches beside Jan, Beryl pointed out the gravesite and showed that in the photographs a board with a riser had leaned against a shed.

She stated her theory: "The belief I have is that she intended to execute the plan on a holiday when she knew everyone was away and she'd have at least a day's time to remain in that back yard grave. She wanted to be sure the kudzu covered the weapon and the rats had time to destroy the evidence." Beryl then described how Greta engineered the suicide to look like a murder.

Gretchen Osterhaus wept. "She must have loved him a great deal to punish him so much for wanting to leave her."

"Yes," Beryl said, "that must have been the reason."

"Will you be making a formal report?" Helena asked Jan.

"Yes," he said quietly.

"And soon? While Miss Tilson is still here so that she gets proper credit for solving this crime? I know you withdrew from the case because he was your father, but the people who failed to see what Miss Tilson saw should have the opportunity to congratulate her on her perspicacity."

"I don't need any congratulations," Beryl said, trying to sound modest instead of irritated.

"First thing tomorrow morning, we'll all meet in the magistrate's office and I'll give a preliminary report," Jan said.

MONDAY, MARCH 26, 2012

Jan and Beryl drove to the magistrate's office and, as expected, found Helena and her daughters waiting outside for them.

Jan commenced to make his informal statement, outlining the new 'alternate theory' which he illustrated with the official crime scene photos and the photos recently taken on their cellphones. "Mr. Adolph Gerber is in agreement with this new version of events. As soon as he's available, he will give his reasons for supporting this version."

The magistrate had already heard of the incident at the campsite. "Are you referring to the leg wound he received at the campsite near Kwamalasamutu?"

"Yes. He's recovering very well. He should be able to walk without crutches in a day or so."

"Does the incident at the campsite have anything to do with this alternate theory?"

"No, Your Honor," Jan said. "Nothing whatsoever. I would like to say that Miss Tilson should be present when the formal declaration is made and that she should be present when the authorities visit the Gerber House crime scene. She will be available to answer any questions an investigatory committee may have. Unfortunately, she has work to do in her home in the United States and cannot easily accommodate a protracted hearing. So the sooner we have the formal presentation, the better. Additionally, both she and I have contracted a stomach flu or case of food poisoning and need a day or two to recover."

"Why don't we arrange for a formal presentation of the theory for Wednesday morning. If Mr. Gerber can appear in person, we'll hear him then. I think that his testimony is vital, too. If he's not prepared, we can postpone the formal presentation until he's ready and ask Miss Tilson either to remain or to return at a later time. Meanwhile, we'll summon all the interested parties."

"That will be fine," Jan said, looking at Beryl for confirmation.

"You and Miss Tilson can take a few days off. Just take your phone with you wherever you go to recuperate." The magistrate smiled knowledgeably.

Dolph called asking that they come to his house immediately. They went directly to the Gerber house and knocked on the door, giving him enough time to answer in the event that he was upstairs when they knocked.

Dolph finally responded to the knock. "I was looking for a baseball bat," he said. "While I was in the shower upstairs, somebody came into the house and went into the music room. That door had been locked; but whoever entered it left it standing open when he left. Upstairs! With me right there in the bathroom!"

"Did they get anything?"

"I don't know yet. Nothing looks disturbed."

Jan told him how the preliminary report went and that Dolph was expected in the magistrate's office on Wednesday morning.

"It's fine with me," Dolph said. "Incidentally, I've thought up a few supportive acts and statements that my mother and Piet made just prior to the suicide. If the good Miss Tilson will make us tea, I'll go over them with you."

He outlined the "parting gifts" and "statements" both his mother and Piet had made that now, in retrospect, made much more sense than they had made at the time.

Jan was still puzzled by the Gerber house break-in. "What could they have been looking for?"

Dolph picked up a sterling silver candlestick. "It doesn't look like a burglary for money or valuables. A coin collection was still in its album inside an open drawer."

"Maybe the entry was made to plant a surveillance device," Jan suggested. "I'll have the house swept for electronic devices." Jan called for the "bug" unit to come. "After they get here, we can go to my place," he said. "It'll take them a couple of hours to finish the job."

When they got back to Jan's apartment, Helena Osterhaus and her daughters were parked outside waiting. "I'm beginning to wish we were back at the campsite," Jan said. "It was more peaceful."

Jan asked Beryl and Dolph to wait in the car. He walked to Helena and asked her to defer answering any questions until the Wednesday session. "I'm not feeling well," he said. "And my companions are also not well. You will simply have to excuse us."

Helena waved her fingers at Beryl and smiled. "Of course, Jan. We really didn't mean to intrude. I simply wanted to warn you that the press has been harassing me for interviews about the preliminary report. I'm sure that sooner or later they'll be after you and," she looked at the car, "your friends. Please let me know if there is anything whatsoever that I can do to help expedite the process."

"Thank you," he said firmly. "Just let the law take its course."

"But if you do think of something, please promise me that you won't hesitate to ask." She started the engine. Jan waited on the sidewalk until they had driven down the street and were out of sight.

Dolph and Beryl followed him into the apartment. No one spoke until he checked the cameras. "It's all clear," he said. Beryl went into the bathroom and closed the door. When she came out again she looked relaxed. Jan asked, "Who is ready for a tall gin and tonic?"

"I am," Dolph said, looking as though he were about to collapse. Beryl called, "Ditto!" as she helped him to sit in a reclining chair in the living room. She turned on the television. Instantly, his eyes closed and he fell asleep.

Jan took his landline receiver off the hook and put his cellphone on 'vibrate.' He turned off all the lights and scrolled through the TV channels until he found a movie.

He sat on the couch and took his shoes off. "Come over here," he softly called to Beryl. She knelt on the couch and he immediately reached out and grabbed her. "You're out of uniform, soldier," he whispered. "That's ten demerits for not wearing your Puss'n'Boots."

"Oh, please," she pleaded, "don't put any black marks on my record." Then they laughed at the absurdity of the entire situation. They began to watch the movie. Within fifteen minutes they, too, were soundly sleeping.

They slept through the evening news, completely missing a reporter's coverage of the "Strange case of suicidal spite" and his interview with Helena Osterhaus.

"Justice will be done," Helena was saying to the camera. "I have longed for my husband's vindication. This is all I ever wanted. Now we can return to the Netherlands and speak his name with pride... and love."

Dolph awakened at seven o'clock. Jan and Beryl were sleeping on the couch. The television was still on. "Hello!" Dolph called, rousing them. "I think it's time for me to go home. And I must say, this is one comfortable chair."

The ice in all three gin and tonics had melted without any of them having taken a sip.

.

As they approached the Gerber House, television news trucks were parked outside. Jan kept on driving. "Let's check into a hotel and eat and spend the night in peace."

No one disagreed.

.

They checked into adjoining rooms and ordered the most delicious, and to Beryl, the most fattening food they could find on the room service menu.

Dolph was in the adjoining single room but Beryl and Jan were in the main double room. They all ate in the larger room and then settled back to play a game Dolph called, "It all makes sense to me now." In this new game, Dolph related how small gifts made by Piet had suddenly loomed large in his mind now that he realized the only explanation that gave significance to their otherwise meaningless and confusing nature, was precisely the explanation given by the 'alternate theory' of the crime.

When he finished, Beryl sighed. "Piet must have been a wonderful man." And then she began to laugh infectiously.

"This is hysterical laughter," Dolph finally was able to say. "Processing something this terrible creates such tension that the only way to relieve it is to laugh idiotically."

"Believe me," Jan said with a sad-clown's insight, "alone... none of us would laugh at all."

Later, when the news came on and they were fully awake, they laughed again to see Helena's interview and hear her rhapsodize about the strange case of suicidal spite.

WEDNESDAY, MARCH 28, 2012

Jan, Beryl, Dolph, and Helena Osterhaus were asked to sit at a small table in front of three elderly gentlemen who composed the judiciary council and to answer questions that seemed, on balance, to be more hostile than cordial.

After having been asked to review the alternate version of the crime from several perspectives, Jan was asked why he had not acted more expeditiously to come to his father's aid. He answered, "Because he was my father and protocol requires that I absent myself from the investigation of family members." The followup question was, "If protocol requires that you absent yourself, why did you get involved at this time when it is too late to help him?"

Helena Osterhaus stood up and begged to be allowed to answer the question. "All along I have begged Captain Osterhaus to solve this most mysterious conundrum; and he always explained that he was not at liberty to get involved in the matter; but it was not until I appealed to him on behalf of his two half-sisters, my innocent daughters, that he had a change of heart. And, after all, the case was closed. My daughters loved their father and he loved them; and it wounded them to hear him referred to in such immoral terms. How could we ever hope for them to marry into good Dutch families when their father was said to be a common criminal? It was because I pressed Captain Osterhaus and begged him to call in a private investigator that he relented and called in Miss Tilson."

Beryl was asked why she was so available "to come so far at a moment's notice." Was she some sort of "Have gun, Will travel" mercenary? She answered that Captain Osterhaus's request was urgent and others in her office were willing and ready to fulfill any duties that she had not completed. "So you responded because overturning a three year old conviction seemed urgent? And if I were to call and describe to you a similar situation, you would fly to another continent?" She answered, "No, I would not." He persisted, "And why not?" She replied, "Because we are not old friends." The questioning had begun to seem silly.

Dolph was asked about his sudden ability to remember actions and remarks that he should have reported to the police at the time. He said, "That Piet Osterhaus gave me a leather jacket and a hunting knife did not seem remotely relevant at the time. That my mother was depressed was already suspected as her reaction to his new will. I attributed her unusual remarks to this cause and not to his intention to leave her and return to his wife and family in Amsterdam. I did sense that she seemed inordinately bitter towards him; but for so long as I believed that he had killed her, I attributed this bitterness to fear and resentment over the will, although, as I've said, it did seem excessively bitter. Yes, bitter. Very bitter."

Again, Helena Osterhaus begged to be allowed to comment. "My husband did not wish to hurt Greta Gerber's feelings any more than necessary. He told me in our phone conversations how unhappy she was that he and I had reconciled. She threatened to create a scandal; and he said that he warned her that he intended to keep our innocent girls free from scandal and that if she persisted in broadcasting the sordid details of their illicit love affair, he would not provide for her and her children."

The widow Osterhaus begged that they overturn his conviction as quickly as possible so that she could take her daughters home and let them rejoin their school classes - "this time with their heads held high." She added. "All I want is the restoration of my husband's good name."

After a few more questions about the camp site, it was determined that, possessing neither gold nor relevance to the present matter, the site did not warrant further scrutiny; and the council adjourned, promising to have its answer by the following morning.

It was nearly three o'clock in the afternoon when everyone left the building.

THURSDAY, MARCH 29, 2012

Beryl and Jan slept until nearly noon. Jan turned on the TV to get the news. "Come see this," he called. "They're on the steps of the courthouse confirming the overturning of Piet's conviction. Now maybe we can all return to normal. Let's go to the beach. It's sunny and I feel like I need an oceanic cleansing."

They packed a lunch and the bathing suits they had bought while staying at the hotel and headed for the beach. They left their phones off while they swam and collected shells. After several hours of being alone, finally, another couple came walking down the strand. "Let's ask them to take our picture together," Beryl said. Jan asked them if they would, and a reciprocal arrangement was made. They took photographs of the couple on the couple's phones and then they posed together while the couple took photographs of them. It was all so pleasant. As they parted company their phones rang. They noticed that they had quite a long list of messages to answer. Jan answered Dolph's call.

"Where have you been?" Dolph asked.

"We're at the beach. Why? What's up?"

"It's been on the news for the past hour. Helena Osterhaus has gotten an attorney and he has just announced that they will be seeking to have all of Piet's property restored to them."

"What?"

"You heard me correctly."

"We'll be right over."

.

There were reporters outside the Gerber House. Jan and Beryl brushed past them and called Dolph's private line, asking that he let them in.

Dolph was watching a newscast. "Take a seat," he said. "After the commercial, we'll see the latest segment of the saga. They intend to take every bit of property Andrea and I now own. Helena met with an attorney who assured her that since my mother contrived to convict an innocent man of her murder, she inflicted enormous injuries, both psychological and financial, upon his legal wife and legitimate heirs. These injuries apparently require a great deal of compensation. And not only that, but she's come into possession of an envelope filled with promissory notes that constitute assets of her late husband's estate. Between owning the debts and being compensated for the injuries, she'll get absolutely everything. I can always get a job, but I'll never be able to get one that will pay for Juliana's medical care."

"So," Beryl asked, "how did they happen to come upon those notes?"

"The break-in," Jan surmised. "They must have been hidden in this house. In the furor over the murder-suicide everybody was so distracted that nobody ever made a competent search of this home or made a list of Piet's assets."

Dolph took a deep breath. "And we never saw this coming."

"This is all my fault," Jan said. "I've inflicted my private grief on you. I don't have much, but I should be able to come up with at least half of Juliana's medical bills. There won't be any gap in her treatment."

Beryl stood up. "Oh, for God's sake. Listen to the two of you. Men. Men are such pussies." She held out her hand. "Give me the keys to the Land Rover and to your apartment."

Jan looked up. "Why? What are you planning to do?"

"Just give me the keys!" He handed them to her. "Stay here," she said, "and keep your phone on in case I call you. Helena is probably still staying at the Trop."

Beryl drove to Jan's apartment, removed a half dozen of the disks from their hiding place, and called the hotel, asking for Mrs. Helena Osterhaus. The hotel regretted that no calls were to be put through to

Mrs. Osterhaus's suite. They also would not give out her room number. Beryl called Jan and asked him to use his influence to get the number and to call her right back. He did. Helena Osterhaus and daughters occupied Suite 427.

Elise, the older daughter, answered Beryl's knock. "My mother is napping and is not to be disturbed," she said through a nearly closed door.

"She wants to talk to me," Beryl said as she pushed the door and the girl aside and strode directly into the bedroom without knocking.

Helena, her face comically plastered with cosmetic mud, protested, "How dare you?"

"I think we need to talk," Beryl replied. "Allow me to show you what you are seeking to show the socialites of Amsterdam." She switched on the television, changed the settings to DVD, and pushed in a disk. Then she closed the bedroom door. "Your daughters may not want to see this now that you've revived the saintly spirit of their father."

Helena Osterhaus watched a few minutes of the recording and sat speechless. Finally, she muttered, "My God!"

"Here," Beryl said, "let me fast forward it." She stopped at intervals, one more disgusting than the next. "Usually Piet wears a mask, but in a few of the scenes," she stopped the rolling images, "such as this, you can clearly see his face. How many of these DVDs would you like to watch? Do you want to see your husband sexually molesting a toddler or would you prefer to see videos of him with a twelve year old? There is a whole catalogue of shows to pick from. After seeing these wretched images, the folks in Amsterdam are not going to invite you to any parties. And I really doubt that they'll be sending their sons to your house, begging to marry into your family."

Helena muffled her scream. "Turn it off!" she gasped. "Get out! Get out!"

"Calm yourself," Beryl said in a low, soft voice. "You wanted help to clear your husband's name for the sake of your daughters. Jan and Dolph, at significant cost to themselves, helped you. The truth of Piet Osterhaus is a terrible burden for the two of them to carry alone; yet, they willingly spared you and your girls from having to bear it. All you had to do was go home and restart your life without having a murderer in the family. Well... I've seen more of these videos and an investigation into Piet's activities is not going to relieve you of that. Murder will be the least of it."

"Why are you doing this to me?" Helena whispered, watching the screen in a "car-wreck" response - unable to look at the images and unable to turn away from them.

"Your attorney should have warned you that no action is undertaken in a vacuum. You will strike something, and what you strike may strike you back." She removed the DVD and inserted another of Piet with the toddler. Helena gasped and covered her eyes. "You might as well look. That little girl is Juliana Gerber and Dolph Gerber is devoting his life to caring for her. Her rehabilitation is expensive. If you bring an action against the Gerbers, your husband's estate will be sued to compensate that little girl for all that he did to her. And these films are not the only evidence against him.

"Call your attorney and withdraw the suits - all of them. And then announce to a news outlet that you are returning to Amsterdam."

"These must be fakes. Piet Osterhaus would never have done such things!"

"Take a good look. These are genuine and if you insist on calling them 'fakes,' we'll take them to the authorities to have them authenticated. Piet's parents will be asked to give their opinion. And they will not thank you for making them give it. In short, the secret of your husband's sadism will become cocktail party chatter in every civilized city that you and your soon-to-be outcast daughters will ever visit. Call your attorney and put an end to a war you cannot win."

"I don't believe this," Helena whispered. "How could he have done this?"

"You probably don't know that Piet reproduced these vile images commercially, and that you and your daughters have been living off the income from pornography. How do you think that information is going to be received?"

Beryl ejected the DVD and placed another one into the player. "Here is another," she said, "that you can watch along with the respectable people here and in The Netherlands who will be wondering what kind of human being you are that you would consider victimizing Juliana Gerber even further."

"I didn't know," Helena began to sob. "Turn it off. Turn it off."

"No. You started this war, and you have got to end it. Call your attorney and a TV station. You're sorry, but you're returning to Amsterdam immediately."

Helena Osterhaus did not reach for the telephone.

"I'm not going to play with you. It won't be up to Dolph or Jan to decide what to do with these DVDs. You've got to deal with me."

Helena Osterhaus brought her legs to the side of the bed and placed her feet on the floor. She did not have to do this in order to reach for the phone. Beryl was prepared when Helena suddenly leaped and tried to snatch the stack of DVDs from her hand. Beryl blocked her arm and struck the woman's chin with the heel of her hand. Then she grabbed Helena's hair and dragged her back to the bed. "You silly woman," she said, more surprised than threatened, "I'm a trained martial artist! Why is that so hard for people to believe?" Then she handed the telephone to Helena. "Call your attorney... now!" Helena's face cream-mud was on Beryl's hand. She took a tissue and wiped it off. "Call!"

Helena looked at a few papers that were on the bed to check for phone numbers. She dialed the number and stammered through the call. "New information has come to light," she said by way of explanation. "I cannot move forward with this case. Please submit a final bill to me. I'm calling the TV people and I'll explain that you have acted with kind professionalism and my decision has nothing to do with your excellent representation of my interests."

Helena's capitulation seemed a little too easy. Beryl watched and wondered what was coming next as Helena called the television station and repeated the facts of her withdrawal of any legal proceedings. "It was all a terrible mistake," she said. "I have asked Mr. Gerber's pardon for instituting this action. I'm withdrawing it now and will be returning to

Amsterdam immediately." She hung up the phone and turned to Beryl. "I've done as you've asked. Now, please go. Just leave me in peace!"

"We are not finished," Beryl said. "I want you to tell me about that private investigator you hired... the one who searched Jan's apartment and Dolph's house. How did he manage to find that envelope of promissory notes?"

"What does that have to do with you? Haven't you caused enough trouble?"

Beryl laughed. "'Trouble'? I've been your Lady Bountiful. I'm the fool who tried to help you. How did he know where to find the notes?"

"You can go to hell!" She wiped her eyes.

Beryl walked to the bedroom door and opened it. "Girls! Your mother would like you to see--"

"No!" Helena shouted to the girls. "You stay out there! She's joking!"

Beryl closed the door. "What all did you hire him to do?" She went to the player and increased the volume. Juliana was shrieking in the video.

Gretchen and Elise pounded on Helena's door. "Mother! What's going on in there?"

Beryl walked to the door. "Do I let them in or are you going to be reasonable?"

"It's nothing!" Helena shouted at the door. To Beryl she pleaded, "Stop it! Just stop playing those videos!" She began to sob again.

"Tell me what all he was looking for. He got the promissory notes from the Gerber House and he also searched Jan's apartment. What was he after?" Beryl insisted.

"Gold maps! All right! Now you know! Gold maps! We knew that Dolph and you went down to a secret placer mine. Dolph stole that map from Piet. We heard that Jan knew where it was, too. The maps weren't just on paper. Piet videotaped his gold mining sites. He told a lot of people that."

"You hired a man to 'break and enter' Jan's home? He's an NBI officer. What did you hope to find? Stolen maps and videos? Promissory notes? At Jan's?"

"Those notes are my property! I'm Piet's widow!"

"The man you hired to break into Dolph's house wasn't there for more than a few minutes. How did he know where to look?"

"I didn't hire anyone. I went myself. And I didn't break in. I had a set of Piet's keys to the house."

"How did you know where to look?"

"My father-in-law told me. Piet was having monstrous headaches and blurred vision and my father-in-law went to see him. He was the last person in the family to see Piet. He told the old man that he had hidden something valuable in the piano. He told him to get it and give it to Jan and Jan would know what to do with it. Jan? What did Jan ever do for his father that he should be rewarded? That was just before Piet died. My father-in-law didn't mention it until a few months ago when he saw how much my girls were suffering."

"Where are the notes now? They are worthless. Get this through your head! The more Piet's estate is worth, the more Gerber will collect for damages he inflicted upon Juliana. You cannot win but you can lose. Your family will be vilified. You will be a laughingstock for having brought this calamity down on yourself."

"Why are you doing this to me?" Helena wept. "I've spent every cent I have just to come here to find some of the property Dolph stole from Piet. I have two daughters to raise. They deserve to be sent to good schools and to have decent clothing and a home of their own. I'm still young... how much longer do I have to live with my in-laws?" She began to sob. "It isn't fair that the Gerbers should get everything. I'm Piet's widow! I'm entitled to something!"

Beryl turned off the television and sat on the bed. "I ought not to trust you. Jan and I tried to help you once and look what that got us! I'll tell you what the gold mine videos were. Those pornographic videos were Piet's gold mine. He joked about it. He made the videos and then traded master recordings of them to gangs of burglars. He melted down the gold from jewelry the thieves stole in a half-dozen countries and pried out the diamonds and other valuable gems and sold them in Colombia for full price. The thieves couldn't get much if they tried to fence the stuff they stole at home, but they made plenty by making copies of Piet's sadism videos. Yes, you were living on the proceeds of filmed sexual torture of children and grown women, too. That was his gold mine." She got up and turned on the television and inserted one of the videos that showed Prego giving the camera to Piet and then torturing the woman. "Put an end to this nightmare. Where are the promissory notes? Please tell me that you didn't give them to your attorney!"

"No," she began to sob, "they're in my purse. I was going to photocopy them and then give him the copies." She looked up at Beryl suspiciously. "You and Dolph... didn't you just go down to a secret placer mine?"

"No. We went down to a played out placer site which is where Piet met the thieves to conduct business. The site was occupied by Piet's partner. This is the man in the film." She took out her iPhone. "I just took these. They're of the site and the man who worked with Piet. He shot Dolph and Jan shot him. The caiman ate his corpse... or so Jan learned when he went to the site two days later."

Helena stared more at the old rusted pieces of equipment then she started at Prego's body. "My God! I almost went there myself! What am I going to do?"

"Give me the promissory notes, and be content that you've salvaged your dignity."

"I can't believe that there's no gold mine!" Helena reached into her purse. Beryl would not have been surprised if she pulled out a gun and started shooting. But she removed only an old envelope crammed with papers. She gave the envelope to Beryl.

"Call the airport and make your reservations," Beryl suggested, handing her the phone.

Helena took the phone and began to whine. She called the airport. KLM had a flight that was leaving for Amsterdam at 7 p.m. Helena booked three seats on it. "We don't have much time," she said, trying to stifle her tears. "Girls!" she called. "We have to start packing right away!" Helena began to wipe her face. "I'll have to hurry. I don't want to miss the flight. I really don't want to face any reporters."

The sun was near the western horizon and the fluffy clouds in the sky were a dozen different shades of pink and gold as Beryl drove along the Waterkant and headed for Dolph's house. The planets were beginning to appear. It promised to be a warm, dry night.

As she pulled up to the curb, the pizza delivery man was just leaving. "Thank God," she said, as she passed him. "I'm starved." She ran into the kitchen to wash her hands.

Jan and Dolph had already begun to scarf down the pizza. "Do you like ham and pineapple pizza?" Dolph asked.

"There is no such thing," Beryl said, pulling out a slice of tomato, cheese and mushroom. "I'm famished."

"Tell us that you watched her plane take off," Jan insisted. "Please tell us that!"

"I did. I stood there and waved goodbye. I helped her to pack and followed her to the airport. She returned her rental car and went to the gate. I went inside and watched them board the plane."

"Did you watch it take off?" Jan wanted to be certain.

"Yes. She's well over the Atlantic even as we speak. Here," she looked at Jan, "is a present for you... the promissory notes Greta signed. Piet wanted you to have them. He told your grandfather to get them and give them to you since you'd know what to do with them." She tossed him the envelope.

Jan looked inside the envelope. "My God! These must total in the hundreds of thousands!" He handed the collection to Dolph. "My compliments."

"Can I buy them from you for the cost of Beryl's expenses, your own invaluable assistance and expense, and just because I want to sleep at night knowing the debts are squared?"

"No," Jan said, "this one's on me."

"Like hell," Dolph said, getting up to get his checkbook. "I'm the one who engaged the services of Wagner & Tilson, and Burnham Publications, and the worst music I've ever heard."

"What is going to happen to the DVD's?" Jan asked.

Dolph shrugged. "On one hand we ought to destroy them... but on the other hand, they're our leverage. I've thought about putting them in a safe deposit box. What should we do? Divide them?"

Jan looked at Beryl. "Let's give them to her. Let her take them home. I trust her."

"I trust her, too. It's ok with me."

"Well," Beryl protested, "It isn't ok with me. I'm not traveling with those pornographic videos on me. The person they belong to is Juliana. In years to come, they may be her only guarantee of compensation. Helena was in shock when she saw them. Anything she said or did after seeing them was compromised. She may get home and decide that she should simply deny the man in the pictures was Piet. For Juliana's sake, Dolph should also preserve those records of the ECT in Peru and those surgical procedures she had done in Sao Paulo. Let Jan take the DVDs of Prego and the women."

She finished eating the pizza. "I'm stuffed. By the way, you might want to redecorate that piano room. The woodwork shows up nicely on film." She sighed. "And I guess my job is finished here. I ought to make reservations for a flight home."

Jan looked up. "Why so soon?" he asked, offended by her decision. "I thought we could spend some time together."

"Will they be days in which we talk about this case? If so, I'll book a flight home right now."

"No. What is that Zen saying? *Burn your good deeds behind you.* Don't expect rewards or accolades because you've done a good deed. I'm burning this whole episode behind me."

Dolph shook his head. "I wish I could. I would start by burning down this whole goddamned house of horror."

"No," Jan said solemnly. "It's not the house's fault."

The cuckoo clock began to strike nine. When the bird finished its announcement, Beryl said slyly, "What you could do..."

Dolph stood up. "Yes. Good idea. And I'm gonna do it now!" He pulled the cuckoo clock off the wall. "Help me," he said to Jan who did not know what he was supposed to do to help.

"There's gasoline in the shed," Dolph said as he exited the back door and went into the garden to unlock the shed. "Bring the promissory notes," he called to Beryl.

Jan got the can of gasoline which Dolph poured over the clock. He lit a match and tossed it onto the clock. As they stood there, watching the flames, Beryl said, "This is probably the stupidest thing I've ever done in my life. But why does it feel so right... so good?"

"Amen," Dolph said. "I should have done this years ago. I see things more clearly now. I'm gonna have the piano room completely redecorated. I may sell the piano... and the house! Actually, I know a smaller and very pretty house that's for sale near Juliana's school. I'll show Juliana. Maybe she'll like it there." He took the envelope of promissory notes and tossed them onto the fire.

While they stood, strangely satisfied by the flames, a little whistle sounded from inside the clock. "Rest in peace, Little Fellow," Dolph said. "Your murderous days are over."

"A nice small house," Jan repeated. "That's not a bad idea. I think I've outgrown my stupid duplex." He grabbed Beryl. "Where would you like to live, Madame Puss'n'Boots?"

"Right now? In Philadelphia."

"No. Right now, it's the Berg En Dal Resort for you." He suddenly picked Beryl up and tossed her over his shoulder in a fireman's carry. "When I began this quest for Piet's good name, I told this woman that I would be spilling my guts. She says, 'Ooooh... I don't want to clean up the messy guts.' It's time she did some secret Puss'n'Boots housekeeping. Dolph, call me next week. If I'm still alive, we can meet for lunch."

-30-